Bound

Eternally Cur

By

Joan De La Haye

www.joandelahaye.com
Cover art by Joan De La Haye
1st Print Edition January 2024

Also by Joan De La Haye

Sliced and Diced Collections

Sliced and Diced

Sliced and Diced 2

Sliced and Diced 3

The Diabolical Series

Shadows

The Veil

The Eternally Cursed Chronicles

Bound by Betrayal

The Race Series

The Race

Training Days

Besieged

Retribution
Consequence
The Patron

Standalone
Fury
Requiem in E Sharp
Burning
Oasis

Watch for more at https://joandelahaye.com/.

Author's note

Dear Readers,

I want to take a moment to address the historical elements present in Bound by Betrayal. While I've drawn inspiration from various historical events, figures, and periods, it's essential to clarify that this work is not intended to be historically accurate. Instead, I've woven elements of history into the narrative to enhance the richness and depth of the world within these pages.

Characters who may bear a resemblance to historical figures are purely products of imagination and should not be taken as accurate representations of the real individuals they may loosely resemble. This story takes place in a fantastical realm with its own rules, cultures, and timelines, distinct from any specific historical reality.

My aim is to transport you into a world of wonder, magic, and adventure. The historical details serve as a backdrop, adding colour to the tapestry of this tale, but they should not be considered accurate reflections of the past.

I hope you enjoy this journey into a realm of fantasy and imagination. Thank you for embarking on this adventure with me.

1

The beep beep beep of the metal detector echoed along the ages and down through the earth, competing with the sounds of the insects and animal life that can only be found on a South African farm. The two boys' excited laughter got louder the faster the beeps came. They'd stumbled onto something. It was the first time they'd found anything with their homemade instrument. They'd discovered the design online and built it in their father's workshop. Their arses had burnt when their father realised they'd cannibalised his lawnmower. But judging by the beeps, they'd hit the motherload.

Sneaking onto their next-door neighbour's farm had been exciting, to begin with, but finding treasure would make any punishment their father would dish out worth it.

Sunlight filtered down through the branches of the ancient Blue Gum trees as Sam handed the spade to his younger brother, Daniel, and said, "It's your turn."

"It's always my turn," Daniel grumbled.

"That's because you're younger and have to do as I say," Sam said as he crossed his arms and nodded. "And if you don't, I'll *make* you, and we both know I can." Sam grinned as the memory of Daniel's last attempt at rebelling against his rule as older brother drifted through his mind. It had the sweet taste of victory to it.

Daniel ignored the self-satisfied grin on his brother's face and started digging.

The spade struck the ancient wood, sending splinters flying.

"What have you hit?" Sam asked, peering down into the hole.

"How the fuck should I know," Daniel said, blushing at his use of the swear word. His mother would have made him put a five Rand coin in the jar if she'd heard him.

"You said the F word." Sam grinned once more at him, this time with pride. "Don't worry; I won't tell Mom."

"You promise?"

"Of course. I would never split on you."

"That's what you said the last time, and I was grounded for a week."

"That wasn't my fault. Dad already knew it was you but was going to ground me if I didn't tell him the truth. I had to tell him. I didn't have a choice," Sam said, spreading his arms out in supplication. "I'm sorry."

"It's cool. Just don't tell Mom I used the F word. I'm saving up to buy Maria something for Valentine's."

"Maria?" Sam frowned. "Really?"

"What's wrong with Maria?"

"Isn't she a little... round?"

"She's not fat."

"Whatever. Let's just get this... whatever it is out of the ground."

Sam took the spade from his little brother and made the hole bigger. Sweat poured down their backs when they uncovered what looked like an old coffin with intricate carvings cut deep into the wood. The wood was rotten and crumbled when they touched it. The desiccated corpse of what they assumed was a woman stared at them through empty eye sockets, her jaw open as though she'd been screaming when she was buried. Strands of copper-coloured hair lay across her skeletal shoulders.

"Fuck," they both said as they looked down at her bones.

"Why'd the machine go off for a bunch of old bones?" Daniel wondered.

"Who knows? Maybe it doesn't work?" Sam said with a shrug.

"But we tested it in the kitchen, and it worked. We now know where Mom puts all the coins we put in the jar."

They stared down at the skeleton. Frustrated frowns creased both their faces.

"What's that?" Daniel asked, pointing at the woman's hand.

Sam bent down and picked up her hand, but her arm came away from the rest of the body.

Daniel giggled like one of the girls in his class and put his dirty hand over his mouth to smother the hysteria building in him.

"That's so gross," Daniel said once he got the giggles under control. "What's she got in her hand?"

"Looks like a huge rusty old nail," Sam said. "Actually, it looks like she's got them nailed into her bones all over the place."

"I guess someone really nailed her," Daniel said with a grin.

"Not funny," Sam said after he finished rolling his eyes at his little brother.

"Should we pull them out?" Daniel asked.

"Ja," Sam said with a nod. "They might be worth something at the junkyard. They also look really old, so we might even be able to take it to one of those shops that sell all those old things."

"You mean that shop Mom likes to go to and that Dad doesn't want her going to because she always spends too much money and always comes home with junk?" Daniel asked.

"That's the one," Sam said. "Did you bring the pliers?".

"Ja, they're in my bike's toolkit," Daniel said.

"But our bicycles are back at the road," Sam said.

"Ja," Daniel sighed.

"Best you get running then," Sam said.

"Why do I have to go?"

"Because I said so, and you were the idiot who left the tools way back there," Sam said.

"Fine," Daniel groaned, climbed out of the grave, and ran back through the bushveld the same way they'd walked. His skinny legs struggled through the long grass. His green shorts collected blackjacks as he went.

Sam watched him from his perch on the sand they'd collected from their excavation. Laughter burst out between his skew teeth when his brother stumbled over tree roots and ploughed face-first into a spider web. Daniel was afraid of spiders, a fact Sam never tired of exploiting. Daniel's figure grew smaller, and Sam tried to ignore his discomfort. He felt as though the empty eye sockets stared at him. He tried turning his back on her, but the sensation of being watched grew stronger.

A brisk wind rustled the leaves of the trees above him. He shivered and rubbed his arms, bringing his knees closer to his chest. The temperature dropped a few degrees. He peered up at the sky through the branches, expecting to see clouds covering the sun. Not a single cloud dotted the endless blue summer sky. The wind picked up some sand from the heap he sat on and blew it back into the grave.

"What the..." Sam said as he jumped off the pile, watched as a dust devil formed where he'd been sitting, and took more of the sand back to the grave. The earth once again covered the skeleton.

"Shit," Sam said, scanning the horizon for his brother, whose small figure in the distance had just reached their bicycles tied to a tree next to the dirt road. Watching his brother, he realised that leaving them there probably hadn't been the smartest thing they could have done. If their father drove past, he'd know exactly what they were doing. But the bush was too dense to ride their bikes through it.

They'd heard stories about their neighbour's farm being haunted and an old gold mine on it that had been deserted because of the ghosts. There were also stories of buried treasure left by the English army during the Boer War.

The ghost stories hadn't scared Sam. He was interested in the gold and the treasure. It had taken a bit of convincing to get his brother to help make the metal detector, but once the promise of buried treasure had come into it, Daniel had come around. Another dust devil picked up another load of sand and deposited it in the grave.

An exasperated sigh escaped Sam's lips as he picked up the spade and dug the sand out again. Every shovel load he managed to scoop out of the grave was replaced by what felt like another two loads.

"That's it," he shouted at the wind. "I'm getting those fucking nails out even if it means I have to use one of these bones to do it."

He scrambled out of the grave and retrieved the discarded arm he'd dropped earlier. "One of these finger bones might be small enough to get under the nail head," he mused out loud as he examined the skeletal arm. The nail firmly wedged in the hand fell to the ground without further help.

The wind howled.

Sam picked up the nail and jumped back into the grave. He decided to start with the nails in her skull and make his way down. Using the tip of the nail from her hand, he began digging the one out between her eye sockets and slightly above where her nose would have been.

He assumed the skeleton was a woman's because of the long strands of hair still attached to the skull, and it just felt like it was female. He didn't know why he thought it, but he just *knew* it was. He also just knew he had to get those nails out of her. He felt compelled. It was as though a soft voice was whispering to him, telling him to get them out. The voice begged him for help. Another voice carried on the wind screamed for him to stop. He ignored the angry, screaming voice and focused on the sad, pleading one. He felt sorry for her. She needed him.

Sam pried and wiggled the nail between her eyes till it flew out after what seemed like an hour, narrowly missing his right eye, but nicked his temple. Blood slowly dribbled down his face and landed on her forehead. The air around him crackled. The wind screamed. Her bones vibrated.

"What the fuck did you do?" Daniel squealed from above. His dirty face peered down at Sam from the edge of the grave.

"I freed her," Sam shouted over the roar of the wind.

2

Eithne stood hidden in the shadows of their hut in the middle of the village, watching Giric, her faithless husband and clan chief, fawning over Mael Muire. The girl was barely old enough to wed, but the rumours that she was with child had already reached Eithne. The other young girls in the village, Mael Muire's friends, had taken pleasure in letting Eithne know that Mael Muire was pregnant with Giric's child, a child that Eithne had failed to give him.

Over the years, she'd given birth to many bairns, but none of them had lived past a moon. Giric blamed her for the loss of their children. Eithne believed there was something darker preventing her children from surviving. They should have been strong like their father. Eithne, too, came from a long line of Chieftains. Her father had been the chief of the neighbouring clan. Their marriage had been forged after a long, bloody war that continued into their marriage bed.

Eithne knew Mael Muire's mother had hoped to wed Giric herself, but when that plan failed, she'd done all she could to destroy Eithne's marriage. Giric had said she was paranoid. Witchcraft was not the reason she couldn't give him children; it was her inferior bloodline. But Eithne knew she'd been cursed. She could feel it in her bones. A woman trained in the ways of the Mother knows these things. She tried to break the curse, but the fates had something else in store for her. And now, the final piece of her old rival and enemy's plan was being put into action. Mael Muire would take her place as Giric's wife.

Eithne wiped hot tears from her cheeks, retreated inside her home's sanctuary, and knelt before her shrine for Cailleach, the Mother Goddess.

"Protect me, Mother," Eithne prayed. "Please, I beg you, give me the strength to defeat those who have cursed me and now wish to take the little I have left. Please, Cailleach, I beg you. Watch over me."

"That old hag won't save you," Giric said as he walked up behind her and gripped her by the throat. "Mael Muire and her family have demanded your body as her dowry. She will give me the children you failed to give me. Our children will guide our clan into the future. They will be strong warriors that will help me fight and defeat the Romans."

"If you kill me, my father and his clan will see that none of your clan survives long enough to fight the Romans," Eithne whispered as she clawed at Giric's strong hands.

"Your father is weak, and so is his clan. That weakness flows through your veins and is why I don't have an heir."

"You don't need to do this. I could leave and live in the mountains on my own. I can return to my father and clan and live the rest of my days as the village hag."

"You only want to return to your father to convince him to fight me again. He might have forced me to marry you, but he's an old man now, and your brothers are too busy dealing with Roman soldiers on their Southern borders. And once Agricola has slaughtered them, no one will stand in my way, not even the Romans."

"If you kill me, you and Mael Muire and all your children and their children will be cursed. I swear it with my last breath."

Giric squeezed tighter. As her vision grew dark, she saw the hooded hag, the Great Mother of all, Cailleach, standing in the shadows, watching her die.

"Cailleach, save me," Eithne whispered with her last breath.

Giric laughed as her body fell at his feet.

"I am finally free," Giric said. "And Mael Muire and her family have their prize."

Sam scrambled up to the safety of the higher ground and perched on the sand heap next to his brother when the wind threatened to bury him along with the woman he hoped would miraculously come back to life. He didn't understand why he thought that would happen, just that it felt right. The brothers watched in shocked silence from the grave's edge as the discarded arm re-joined the rest of the skeleton and started sprouting veins, ligaments, and bits of muscle. The wind seemed to howl in more profound pain as muscle and skin grew on the bones.

When eyes appeared in the empty sockets, and more hair grew on the skull, the wind became nothing more than a defeated whimper.

"That's gross," Daniel said.

"No, she's not," Sam said. "She's magnificent, and I saved her."

"Are you crazy," Daniel said as he slapped the back of Sam's head, enjoying being the smarter brother for a change. "We can't take her home. How do you think Mom will react to us bringing home some Zombie chick you brought back from the dead, huh?"

"She's not a Zombie," Sam said.

"Then what is she?" Daniel said, squinting down as the corpse continued to reanimate.

"She's beautiful," Sam said.

"She's dirty and naked," Daniel said. "And she looks like Mom."

"Does not," Sam said as he smacked his brother on the back of his head. "Take that back."

"I'm sorry, your Zombie is an old woman who looks like Mom does without her makeup and before she's had her coffee," Daniel said.

Before Sam could respond with his fists, the woman in the grave screamed as she sat up, giving both boys a big enough fright that they fell back and rolled down the sand.

Another figure shimmered on the edge of the grave, giving the boys another fright.

"Do you see that?" Sam shouted and pointed.

Daniel only nodded and tried not to piss himself.

"Zombies and Ghosts," Sam whispered. "I'm never sleeping again."

"I thought you said she wasn't a zombie," Daniel said, not knowing where to look or what to think or say. He knew he should run but couldn't get his legs to move.

"Shut up," Sam shouted for no reason other than making him feel like he was still tough and in control. Like his brother, he knew he should run but couldn't get his legs to cooperate.

The woman now stood in front of them. Neither had seen her move. One second, she had still been screaming in her grave; the next, she was in front of them, wholly restored and naked. Her long, copper-coloured hair seemed to float on the breeze.

"Okay, you're right," Daniel said. "She doesn't look like Mom."

"Told you she was beautiful," Sam said as he took in every inch of her. She was the first woman he'd ever seen naked in the flesh. He'd only seen a naked woman when he snuck a peak when his Dad watched Pornhub and didn't think either of his sons was around. The sight of her caused the same physical reaction to the things he'd seen on Pornhub.

"Dude," Daniel said. "Do you have a boner right now?"

"Like you don't?" Sam said, still not tearing his eyes away from her boobs.

The shimmering figure now stood next to her. The two boys hardly noticed the apparition or the large, rusted iron nails that had begun to shake on the ground where they'd left them. Their fear was temporarily suspended in the wake of their hormones surging through their young and inexperienced brains.

Only when the first nail seemed to drift up like a feather on the breeze and flew through the air like an arrow or a bullet and narrowly missed Sam's head did the instinct for self-preservation kick in.

The naked woman's painfilled screams mingled with the boys' as one of the nails plunged into her shoulder while another grazed her thigh. The shoulder where the ancient nail protruded began to decay and revert to its withered form. When she tried to pull it out with her other hand, the fingers on that hand also began to decompose. She screamed even louder, but not just in pain. The wails that escaped her lips were also filled with frustration.

"I have to help her," Sam shouted over the roar of the wind and the woman's screams.

"Are you insane," Daniel shouted. "We need to get out of here."

"I can't leave her," Sam said, more to himself than anybody else, as he stood up and dodged another nail. He felt the ghostly apparition glare at him. Then the wind picked up and almost pushed him back to the ground, but he fought back with all his boyhood energy. He felt like one of those heroes from the movies he and Daniel loved to watch rescuing the damsel in distress.

He held his hands up as he approached the screaming woman, who looked worse with every passing second. He hoped she knew he was there to save her. Luckily, she wasn't much taller than him as he reached up and pulled the nail out of her shoulder. The moment the poisonous nail was out of her body, she began to heal.

As more nails flew towards her, Sam's immortal Goddess ran for her life. The ghost, the wind, and the nails followed her, leaving the two boys behind.

"I'm going after her," Sam said moments before his little brother tackled him to the windswept ground.

"No, you're not," Daniel said as he used all his strength to pin his brother down. "You're going to let the Zombie chick and the ghost fight it out without us."

"Get off me," Sam shouted as he tried to push Daniel off him.

"If you run off after them, I will tell Mom that you left me alone in the veld to be attacked by a very human *Tsotsi.*"

"Come on," Sam said as he stopped fighting, knowing that his mother's wrath would be far worse than never seeing his Goddess again if he left his baby brother alone. "That's not fair."

"I'm saving your life. That thing with the nails was not fucking around. You can thank me by carrying everything back to our bikes," Daniel said with a grin.

"How are we going to explain this to Dad," Sam said, looking down at their broken metal detector. "That ghost must have broken it when it was throwing a tantrum with the wind."

"We lie," Daniel said with a nod.

"Yep," Sam said. "We lie. Besides, they wouldn't believe us even if we told them."

"Adults," Daniel said. "They have such limited imagination. They wouldn't know the truth if it smacked them right in the face."

"Yep," Sam said as he started picking up all the bits and pieces of their destroyed experiment. "Fucking adults."

"At least we know that worked," Daniel said, looking at the parts his brother had already picked up. "Maybe we should rebuild it."

"Not worth the risk," Sam said. "Who knows what other monsters are buried out there? Probably best we leave them there."

"Good point," Daniel said as he picked up the rest of their tools.

The two boys walked back slowly towards their bicycles in silence, knowing they would never forget the woman they'd brought back from the dead, nor the ghost that had almost killed them. They also knew that once they got home, their father would punish them, and they would probably not sit comfortably for a few days, but it had all been worth it.

3

The early morning sunlight slithered through the slim gaps in the roof's thatching and between the timber slats of the walls. As it progressed on its never-ending journey across the sky, its tendrils of light touched Eithne's bare feet and travelled up her dead limbs, slowly bringing back life into her bones.

The old hag and Great Mother, Cailleach, stood in the shadows and watched her work take hold within Eithne's corpse. She smiled as Eithne took her first breath of immortality. There would be few things in this world that could harm her in the future. No man would ever be able to hurt her again. Eithne would now have power over all men in physical strength and mental acuity. The bloom of her youth had been restored, and she would never age. Her beauty would enslave men. The only thing Cailleach could not give her back was the ability to have children. That was a curse not even Cailleach could undo. But considering she would live forever, not watching her children die would be a blessing, or so Cailleach told herself. She only hoped Eithne would come to see that in time.

Eithne opened her eyes and saw the old hag watching her from the shadows. There was a brief moment of fear, as any creature would feel when beholding great power. Unlike many of her kind, she resisted that fear and only felt gratitude for the Great Mother. She knew it was only thanks to Cailleach's mercy that she was resurrected.

Cailleach knew that the memories of her death at her husband's hands the night before had created blazing anger in her heart. It would never be extinguished. Perhaps it would be lessened with his blood on her hands.

"I have given you a great gift," Cailleach whispered out of the dark. "Be careful what you do with it." With those words drifting on the hazy sunbeams, Cailleach disappeared, leaving Eithne to her own devices and choices.

She ran through a field she didn't recognise, away from the boys who spoke a language she didn't understand. The long, stick-like grass, which was so different to the green grass and heather of the Highlands, whipped her naked legs as she fled from the wind spirit. Nothing made sense. Even the trees seemed foreign to her. She felt as though she was out of step with time.

Flashes of memory whispered on the edge of her vision but were gone as quickly as they came. The terrain changed, and a dusty path resembled what the Romans had used to travel on but seemed of a lower standard than the Roman roads, which wound their way through the land. It was wide enough for a wagon to travel on but was rough and bumpy. A wagon would soon break a wheel on it. Perhaps this strange place didn't have wagons. Perhaps they were horse people.

She followed the path. Running on the track was easier than through the strange field with its long grass. The wind spirit trailed behind her and seemed to lose strength. While it grew weaker, she got stronger and faster. All she knew was that the iron the wind carried could harm her. As long as she kept running and kept the iron at bay, she could discover where she was and regain the memories she'd lost.

The path ended at what appeared to be a black road far superior to anything the Romans had built. It wound up towards and through a distant mountain pass like a black river. A rumbling noise came from where the road disappeared into the mountain. It sounded like rolling thunder. A few moments later, a strange carriage came toward her. It was faster than any wagon she had ever seen. Within minutes, it had passed her. The people inside it stared at her as though she was the one who was cavorting with the Sidhe.

"It's called a car," she heard a disembodied voice say.

Using her second sight, she saw a woman with raven hair through the shimmering haze next to her. She resembled someone she knew she'd once known but couldn't remember from where. She also felt an instant dislike for her but couldn't understand why.

"Where am I?" she asked. "This is not Caledonia."

"No," the spirit replied. "This is a place they call South Africa."

"When am I?" she asked.

"You've been asleep for almost two thousand years."

The shock of where and when she found herself made her knees buckle. She wanted to scream and cry but couldn't remember what she'd left behind or what was worth crying over from before she woke up. The ground beneath her knees felt real, as did the earth she dug her hands into. If it was real, then so was she. She was alive, and that was all that mattered.

"Why don't I remember who I am or what happened to me? I remember some things but not others. I can remember home, the Romans, and my village, but other memories are beyond my grasp."

"Give it time," the spirit said. "You'll remember everything soon. Unfortunately." The last word was barely above a whisper.

Before she could ask anything else, another strange creature roared down the black path. It was different from what the spirit had referred to as a car. It had two wheels, and the man straddling the beast resembled the warriors from her home, except for his strange helmet. Was he riding into a battle on his own, she wondered.

"This should be interesting," the spirit said as the man stopped in front of them and removed his helmet.

He resembled one of the Roman soldiers who'd attacked her village. She remembered the battle as though it had only happened a few months ago. If she'd had a sword, she would have run him through. But the markings on his body were so much like the ones the warriors from her father's clan painted on their bodies. The combination confused her.

"Are you okay," he asked as he climbed off his metal horse and looked her up and down.

She stared at him dumbly. She couldn't fathom why she understood him. She knew he spoke in a language she shouldn't understand. It had been the same with the two boys at her grave. She'd known what they were saying but that they were speaking in a strange tongue. The memory of Cailleach standing over her as she died flashed through her mind, and she understood that one of the gifts she'd received that morning had been the gift of language.

"Are you hurt?" He asked as he walked towards her, looking around as though looking for someone else. "Are you alone out here?"

She wasn't sure how to answer since she was neither hurt nor alone in the strictest sense. Only iron seemed to be able to cause her any real pain, and she suspected the spirit who now stood beside her was the one who had attacked her and tried to keep her buried. She doubted this mortal man could see the ghost. Unable to trust that she could speak his language, she shook her head in response.

"Let's get you somewhere safe," he said as he removed an item of clothing and wrapped it around her naked shoulders. It was the kindest thing any man had ever done for her. The leather was the finest she'd ever felt and was lined with rich, soft linen that felt wonderful against her naked flesh.

Following his lead, she straddled his silver steed. It felt as though a hundred horses galloped beneath her. She hadn't felt anything like it before. She burst out laughing from the pleasure.

"First time on a bike?" He said, looking over his shoulder as he put his strange helmet on.

For a brief moment, she wondered if he was taking her into battle with him as some trophy to show his men, but a man who had been as gentle with her as he had been would never do such a thing. He was so unlike the men from her tribe or her husband. A memory stirred as she clung to her rescuer's waist.

"Shit," the spirit said. "Here it comes."

4

Eithne stood up and felt the power spread through every part of her. It flooded every sinew and every cell of her entire being. There was nothing she couldn't do. The bruises left by Giric the night before vanished. He would never be able to hurt her again. He would be the one who would feel what it was like to cower. He would feel the fear he had instilled in her every day of their marriage. He would know what it was like to have his life slowly wrung out of him.

The sounds of wedding celebrations drifted on the breeze from the village. They hadn't even waited to bury her first. They'd just left her body in the corner to be eaten by maggots and rats. Deeper and more poignant anger than she had ever felt intermingled with the magical power Cailleach had gifted her, giving her even more strength than the Mother Goddess could ever have imagined. Sparks of energy like small thunderbolts fluttered on her fingertips as she struggled to control the magic.

She screamed as the power overwhelmed her and exploded out of her. When she opened her eyes, the walls of her home no longer stood. All around her was destruction. Her furniture and belongings were nothing but ash. Walking through the detritus of her former life, she made her way toward the village and the ongoing celebrations.

As she walked through the village, she experimented with her abilities. She played with lightning as though it were a toy. She created it in her hands and moulded it into a blue-white ball. She then threw it at the homes of Giric's supporters as though she were Taranis, the God of thunder himself. Houses smouldered and burned in her wake. The village cats followed her as though she were their Queen. When she reached the village square and the wedding party, most of the village was in flames.

Mael Muire was the first to see her. Rage twisted her young face. Eithne was reluctant to admit she was quite beautiful even when hate made her features cruel. There was nothing gentle or kind about Mael Muire or her family. Perhaps that was what made her so attractive to Giric. He had seen her kindness as a weakness. But now he would know that she was anything but weak.

"I thought you killed her," Mael Muire hissed at Giric.

"She was dead when I left her last night," Giric said. His voice sounded weaker and somehow older than Eithne had ever heard him before.

"She's a witch," Mael Muire screamed at the clansmen. "Kill her."

Mael Muire's brothers grabbed their swords while Giric's honour guard picked up their spears and threw them at her. None of them found their mark, even though they were all expert marksmen. Arrows flew at her from all directions but splintered mid-flight.

Eithne smiled as she let her lightning bolts loose on the men of the tribe. They screamed as they burned. Giric stood alone in front of the druid performing their hand-fasting ceremony. Mael Muire and her mother ran for the safety of their hut. It didn't matter to Eithne. She would get them later. The druid was the only one who didn't seem interested in harming Eithne. He bowed his head and walked away, leaving Giric to face her and the consequences of his betrayal.

She felt a moment of regret when one of the clan members she had thought of as a friend burned alongside those who were attacking her, but then another member of the clan ran at her with a sword, ready to kill her. He, too, found his death as she defended herself against his attack. He had been someone she had always been friendly with. When his family had been sick, she had tended to them. Now, he looked at her with so much hate. She had never seen so much hate in another's face, especially not directed at her. Was no one in the village on her side? Did they all see her as an outsider? Did they not realise that she was the one who had been wronged? Had they always felt this way about her, or had they been bewitched by other forces?

In a moment of self-reflection, she turned and surveyed the damage she had done to the village. In some way, she could understand why they might be angry with her for burning their homes, but the moment they chose to stand by Giric as he married another a few hours after killing her, they sealed their fate and deserved to burn with him.

"So, the old hag saved you after all," Giric said as he fell to his knees in front of her.

"She did," Eithne said as she wrapped her hands around Giric's neck.

Her power tingled through her fingers, and burn marks appeared where they touched his skin. She burned him slowly.

His pain-filled screams drowned out the sounds of the village burning and his clan members' screams as they tried to escape the flames. She smiled as the ashes from his body drifted on the wind.

She didn't notice Mael Muire and her mother behind her. She didn't hear their chants until she felt her power weakening. She felt the spear thrust through her and saw her blood on the iron spear's head as it burst through her stomach.

"How?" Eithne whispered as she fell to her knees in front of Giric's burnt husk.

"This spear has been crafted from iron that has been cursed by my mother," Mael Muire said as she twisted the blade to cause Eithne even more pain. "And now that the interfering old hag has made you immortal, we can't just kill you as we had hoped Giric had done for us."

"Bring the box," Mael Muire said to her mother. "We need to hurry."

"Only a few of our people have survived," her mother said.

"They will have to be enough," Mael Muire said with another twist of the blade. "We will need all of them to put her in the ground and keep her there. We can't have her interfering."

With the memory came the pain. She felt the spear twisted in her guts as though it was still there. She forgot to hold on to her Roman rescuer and felt herself being pulled away from him by the wind and a force stronger than anything she'd felt while riding a horse. She found herself flying backwards and landing on the black, hard surface. Her body should have been broken in several places, and she should have been in agony, but she felt no pain, only mild confusion as she stared up at the sky.

"Really?" the spirit said as its hazy form looked down at her. "Not even a broken bone?"

Eithne didn't have time to wonder at the spirit's words or her reasons for wanting to harm her. However, she did notice some resemblance to Mael Muire. They both had the same raven hair and the same eyes. The Roman returned on his metal steed with a roar of thunder.

"What the fuck?" He said as he climbed off his steed and removed his helmet. "Are you okay?"

Eithne bounced back onto her feet and took in her unscathed body. She remembered falling off her horse as a child and how close she'd come to death, the pain of the broken bones and those bones being reset. It had been agony. Her mother had prayed to Cailleach for days, while her father had refused to enter their hut until he knew if she would survive. Once they knew she would live, there had been fears that she would never walk again. Her mother had sworn that it had been Cailleach who had saved her then. The old Hag, as Giric had called her, had been watching over her all her life. And now, once again, Cailleach's gift had saved her.

"How are you not injured?" her handsome Roman asked. "At the very least, you should be covered in road rash."

Eithne shrugged. She still didn't trust herself to speak in his tongue. She also didn't know what her voice would sound like or if she could talk after having been in the ground for many centuries.

"I think we need to get you to a hospital," he said with a blend of worry, confusion and a slight tint of fear. The same mix of emotions was also stamped on his face.

"No!" The spirit screamed in her mind. "No hospitals or doctors. They'd realise something wasn't right with you, and you'd end up being used as a lab rat, and then they'd discover that there is more to the world than their limited interpretation of science, which would not be good for any of us."

Eithne didn't understand everything the spirit was yelling about but did understand that she couldn't go where her rescuer wanted to take her. She shook her head and took a step away from him. She also gestured with her hands that that wasn't an option.

"No doctors, huh?" He said. "You running from someone?"

Eithne nodded, even though she wasn't entirely sure if she was still running from something since the spirit now stood beside her. Running from her seemed pointless. But if telling him she was trying to escape something meant he wouldn't take her to the hospital, she would tell him exactly what she needed to get what she wanted.

"Well," he said, looking around to make sure there wasn't anybody else around. "Let's get you somewhere safe." He climbed back on his silver steed and waited for her to climb on behind him.

"Maybe don't let go of me this time, okay?" He said.

Eithne nodded as she climbed behind him and wrapped her arms around his waist. His steed vibrated between her thighs, creating sensations she hadn't felt riding ordinary horses and had only felt slightly with Giric when he'd taken her. Giric had been a rough and selfish lover. He'd never given her pleasure. She enjoyed the feel of the man's muscles under his shirt and the throbbing sensation rising between her legs. She wanted to laugh and shout and scream all at the same time. She'd never experienced anything like it. She wanted more.

They roared past settlements and dwellings, unlike anything she'd ever seen before. Everything was noisy, and the carriages varied in appearance and size. Even the people she saw along the way were different from what she'd known. Their clothes were so strange. Her senses and brain were overloaded as she tried assimilating all the information she was absorbing. They briefly stopped at the entrance to something that would have been fit for a castle. She'd been right to go with him. He must be a Prince or a Knight to live within the walls of such a Palace. He tapped an odd-looking disk against another strange device, and the gates opened for them. Was he a Magus?

She felt the spirit sigh next to her. Eithne had hoped she'd left the ghost behind, but they were clearly attached somehow.

"We're stuck with each other," the spirit said. "Unfortunately."

5

A storm cloud formed over what was left of the village, and lightning struck the ground next to Mael Muire, missing her by a hair's breadth. Even though the ground absorbed the blast, a shockwave trembled through Eithne and into the spear, protruding from her stomach, causing Eithne to howl in pain. Mael Muire smiled.

"That was a warning, my child," her mother whispered so only Mael Muire and Eithne could hear. "Are you sure you want to do this? The Goddess is not on our side."

"The old hag has had her time, and she's only harming her little pet. There is another new God that has come to our shores that is stronger, and if we want to survive, Mother, we must do his bidding."

"Have you sold your people to the invaders?" Eithne asked through clenched teeth. "How could you betray us all to the Romans? The other tribes will never submit to them."

"The other tribes are weak and roving packs of dogs. The Romans will annihilate us all if we don't submit to them," Mael Muire said with another twist of the spear. "I'm saving my tribe."

"Giric would never have agreed to that," Eithne said as she tried to smother another wave of pain. "He hated the Romans and would have fought them till the end. Surrender would never have been something he would have agreed to."

"You're right," Mael Muire said. "He would never have agreed to my plan, but now he's dead. Thanks to you. I no longer need to deal with him interfering in my plan. Now, I must only deal with you and ensure you never rise again."

"Rise again?" Eithne asked. "I don't understand."

Mael Muire laughed, causing the spear to move even more inside Eithne.

"No," Mael Muire said once she'd stopped laughing. "You wouldn't understand. There are many things you have never been able to comprehend."

"We're ready," her mother said as she reverently held up an ornate chest for the remaining warriors of the tribe to behold. Mael Muire nodded and gestured for two men to take hold of Eithne.

"Don't be concerned," Mael Muire said when they hesitated. "She's been weakened by the iron. Her powers can't save her now, nor can she stop us."

With a single nod, they each grabbed Eithne's arms while Mael Muire slowly withdrew the spear. Eithne howled in pain, and Mael Muire laughed. They dragged her to a coffin that Eithne hadn't seen them carry. She hadn't been aware of any craftsman in the village who had the skill to craft anything like it, nor had she seen anyone making it. She would have marvelled at its intricate designs if they hadn't planned to put her in it while still alive. Then she noticed the curse spelt out in that intricate web of runes.

"Put her in the box," Mael Muire shouted as Eithne struggled against the men holding her.

Their fingers dug into her withering flesh. She could feel her strength being leeched out of every cell in her body.

"Look at her," Mael Muire said. "She's ageing with every breath she takes. Soon, she'll be nothing but bones."

The men lifted her and threw her into the coffin as though she weighed nothing at all. She tried to lift herself out of it once they'd let go of her, but she didn't have the strength to move.

"Give me the nails," Mael Muire commanded.

Eithne watched in frozen horror as Mael Muire smiled triumphantly and held up an ornate hammer engraved with runes resembling the ones from the design on the coffin.

"With these iron nails, I curse you, Eithne, for all eternity." Mael Muire placed the tip of an iron nail on her brow, between her eyes and struck. It pierced her skull. Eithne didn't even have the strength to scream.

"These nails will imprison you in your dying flesh and bones, unable to move or speak." Another nail was placed at the base of her throat. She felt her breath and blood gurgle as she struggled to inhale.

"You will not be able to use any of the gifts bestowed upon you by the mother Goddess, Cailleach." Another nail was hammered through her heart. Eithne didn't feel the rest of the nails being hammered through her hands, feet, stomach, and womb. She watched, unable to move or scream, as they placed the coffin lid over her. Eithne was left alone, screaming silently into the dark.

Somewhere during those centuries in the dark, Eithne lost herself and her memories. She'd slept and forgotten, but now she was awake and remembering, and with those memories came a burning rage. But the kindness of this stranger, who looked like the Romans who had invaded her home and whom Mael Muire had aligned herself with to destroy everything Eithne had loved and held dear, made Eithne wonder if things might be different in this new world. Perhaps she could start a new life and let the memories of the past stay in the past.

They stopped in front of a tall building with many windows. She heard children laughing and music playing, but it was all so different to anything she'd ever heard. The music had depth and a magical sound. There was still the beating of drums and singing, but other instruments were intermingling with what she could recognise. In some ways, it was a cacophony, and she wanted to cover her ears and block out the noise, but another part of her revelled in the newness of it all.

She looked around in awe at the splendour of the buildings around her. They were what she'd imagined the castles she'd heard they had in the South in cities like Londinium looked like. Only this place was cleaner. She couldn't help but wonder where all the animals were. Where did they keep their cattle and sheep? Where did they grow their food? The only sign of animal life was a dog barking and a well-fed cat strolling past. The cat stopped prowling in the middle of the road and changed direction. It headed straight for her and then sat in front of her, waiting for her to pay it some attention.

"That's strange," her Roman said. "That fucking thing hates everyone."

Eithne bent down to stroke it. The cat started purring and rubbed its head against her fingers.

"Come with me," he said. "Let's get some clothes on you before someone sees you and throws me out of the complex."

Eithne followed him, and the cat followed her. She followed him up perfectly even stairs. As they went, she trailed her fingers along the smooth surface of the dwelling and marvelled at the engineering. The Romans must have conquered the world and perfected their building techniques while she slept. The thought that her people had been destroyed brought a wave of emotions that threatened to overwhelm her. She tried to swallow the pain of everything she'd been through and lost, but her body wouldn't obey. The tears came whether she wanted them or not.

"Hey," he said. "It's okay. You're safe. I don't know what happened to you, but you're safe now. I'm not going to hurt you. I promise I'm one of the good guys. Okay?"

The look of concern on his face only made her more emotional. Sobs wracked her body, making it almost impossible to keep walking.

"Fuck!" he said. "It's just a little further. Okay. Please stop crying. My neighbours will think I've done something to you, and then security will be here, and they'll call the cops, and you don't want that, do you?"

Eithne managed to shake her head. The cat rubbed itself against her naked calf and purred.

"Fucking weird," he said with a shake of his head as he looked down at the purring cat.

Eithne shrugged.

"This is a great idea," the spirit said.

Eithne had the distinct impression that the spirit didn't believe this to be a great idea; she would probably be far happier if Eithne were still buried with those cursed nails inserted all over her body.

"This is me," he said, putting a key in the door lock with 69 on it. "It's a great number, don't you think?"

Eithne did not understand his meaning. Was he into numerology? Was he a Druid?

"Okay," he said as he opened the door. "Never mind. Forget I said that."

The spirit giggled, confusing Eithne even more.

"Look," he said as Eithne stepped inside. "Excuse the mess, but I wasn't expecting any company." He picked up a few items of clothing from the floor and what Eithne assumed was something one sat on. It looked far more luxurious than anything she had ever seen before. He must be royalty to have this level of luxury in his rooms.

"I think I've got something you can put on. My girlfriend..." he paused and looked embarrassed as he combed his fingers through his thick black hair. Eithne found herself wondering what his hair would feel like between her fingers. "I mean ... my ex-girlfriend left some clothes here which should fit you."

He disappeared down a short but brightly lit passage and returned a few minutes later with strange items made of cloth that resembled his own but were smaller.

"These should fit," he said as he held them up to her. "You can put them on in the bathroom. It's just down the passage on the right, opposite the bedroom. You're welcome to have a shower while you're in there. You might want to wash all the dirt off your body and hair. It looks like whoever had you buried you alive."

Eithne nodded and clutched the garments to her as though they were the most precious items in the world. She was also afraid someone would take them from her.

"Wait," he said as she was about to walk in the direction he had pointed in. "Did they bury you alive?"

Eithne nodded again and walked towards the chamber he called a bathroom.

"Fucking hell," he said softly. It was almost a whisper. Eithne felt his eyes on her as she walked away from him. "We need to call the cops. I know they're fucking useless, but we should do something, shouldn't we?"

Eithne paused at the entrance to the bathing chamber and looked back at him. She shook her head, walked into the room, and closed the door behind her.

6

Maretta looked down at the cursed sarcophagus passed down through generations of women in her family. For almost 2000 years, her family had been its guardians. All because one of her ancestors had the ill-advised notion to form an unholy pact with the Romans. For a brief time in history, her clan had thrived, even been close to the throne, but the Romans adapted. Her clan did not. The Romans turned their empire into a religion and left her ancestors to fend for themselves, forgetting their promises. She couldn't blame the Romans for abandoning her ancestors. They hadn't delivered their end of the bargain. Scotland had never surrendered to Roman rule.

Looking down at what had become a massive boulder hanging around her neck, Maretta didn't think it was worth it. Mael Muire's ambition had cursed not just Eithne but all of Mael Muire's female descendants. Her brothers could live as they pleased, but Maretta would always be saddled with that damned box. She also had to have a daughter to carry on the legacy of keeping watch over a corpse. It was ridiculous, and she hated her mother for making her do it, but the alternative was far worse. The thought of what would happen if Eithne woke up gave her nightmares.

"Are you coming?" Roger shouted from the door. "The ship won't wait for you."

"Coming, Darling," she called back with one last glance over her shoulder at the coffin. Roger had no idea what was in the box, just that it had to go wherever she did. He knew it was a family heirloom and that it was ancient. He also had the sense not to ask her questions about her family or the box and referred to it as her Kist.

It would take ninety days from Liverpool to the Cape of Good Hope. She'd known that being a soldier's wife would not be easy when she accepted Roger's proposal. They only allowed her to travel with Roger because she was also a field nurse. The war in South Africa was not going well, and they needed all the medical help they could get. The Boer soldiers were putting up a stronger resistance than expected.

Roger was impeccably dressed in his uniform as he waited impatiently for her at the door. His sophisticated air and looks belied his inner nature. She wished she'd known his true nature before their wedding. But she'd never truly had a choice in marrying him. He'd been her mother's choice, not hers.

Their luggage and that infernal box would be brought to the docks in another carriage. She worried about leaving the Kist unattended. What if someone got curious and decided to take a peek inside? There were so many what-ifs. None of her ancestors knew what would happen if Eithne woke up, rose, or broke the curse. Maybe it wouldn't be that bad. There were so many times when Maretta thought about just opening the box herself and pulling all those nails out, but then she thought about all the women who had come before her who had resisted the urge to open it. She thought about her mother's warning. She thought about her mother's story about what Eithne had done to Mael Muire's village on that fateful day. She shuddered at the thought of what Eithne could do to innocent people. No one should be immortal and *that* powerful.

"Are you all right, my dear?" Roger peered at her over the rim of his spectacles. "You look a little pale."

"I'm fine, my love," Maretta said as she reached her gloved hand out to him. "Just nervous about the journey."

"These sea journeys are quite arduous. More so for women, I would think. Are you sure you want to join me? Africa is a harsh continent, and the battlefield is no place for women."

"I am a nurse, Darling," Maretta said, ignoring his condescending tone. "I also doubt Lord Kitchener would look favourably on us if I changed my mind just before departure."

"True, my dear," Roger said with a nod as he finally took her hand. "And you are a credit to your sex."

"What the bloody hell is in this thing," one of the young Cadets in Roger's battalion charged with carrying the Kist to the wagon grumbled as he struggled under its weight.

"Be careful with that," Maretta said. "It's a priceless artefact."

"Yes, Milady," the other Cadet said with laboured breath.

"Does that thing have to come with us?" Roger asked as he watched the men struggle down the stairs.

"It goes where I go. My family has been responsible for protecting the contents for centuries. You knew that when you married me, Darling."

"Yes, dear," Roger said. "But isn't it yet another reason to consider remaining here where you and that thing will be safe."

Maretta released his hand as she took a deep breath and exhaled. It gave her the time to think and collect herself. She'd pay for it later in private if she said the wrong thing. He would never strike her where the bruises would be seen by others, only in areas where her dresses covered her skin completely, which gave him many options. He seemed to enjoy whipping her back and buttocks the most. The only place he never hit her was her face, although sometimes he seemed tempted by the thought. He claimed it was to tame her wild ways, that it wasn't for his pleasure, but he was always engorged while he corrected her behaviour, as he put it.

"Darling," she said with a smile that she hoped looked sincere. "I would rather risk the ire of my ancestors than face a day without you."

"Very well, Dear," he said with a nod. "That thing won't get itself on the carriage. Cadets, you best get moving. The train to Liverpool waits for no man."

Maretta sighed with relief. The thought of staying behind and never seeing the man she loved again was a fate she couldn't bear. Alastair waited for her on the Dark Continent. She only hoped he was still alive.

Eithne stood in the bright room. The white surfaces gleamed and were smooth to her touch.

"Oh! For God's sake. It's just a bloody bathroom and not a particularly nice one," the spirit said. Water miraculously started pouring out of something in a smaller chamber.

"Magic," Eithne whispered. Her voice sounded strange to her ears after not having spoken for almost two thousand years.

"It's a shower. Just get under the water and wash. It's not that complicated, and it certainly isn't magic."

"How did they get the water to come out of that?" Eithne whispered as she crawled around the room, trying to investigate all the different pipes.

"How would I know," the spirit said. "I'm not an engineer, now, am I?"

"What's an engineer?" Eithne said a little above a whisper, enjoying the sound of her voice and being able to speak.

"Oh, for heaven's bloody sake," the spirit hissed. "Just get in the bloody shower."

She removed the first garment he'd given her and climbed under the water. She squealed with delight as the hot water hit her skin.

"This new world is magical," she said as the water washed away centuries of dirt and grime.

She spotted a variety of bottles that looked to contain thick liquids. Did even mere mortals make potions now? It took her a few tries to open the bottles—everything smelt of fresh flowers.

"It's just shampoo and body scrub," the spirit sighed. "You use them to wash your hair and body. They're not magical potions that he brewed. He bought them at a shop, like everyone else."

"Whoever brewed this must be a powerful witch," Eithne said with reverence as she breathed the scent and luxuriated in the feel of the hot water and the liquid soaps as she washed herself with soap and water for the first time in her life. If this was indeed a simple thing to these mortals, she couldn't wait to experience everything else they took for granted. Her future held so many exciting possibilities.

7

The smell of the ocean drifted on the breeze as they set sail. Maretta's stomach rolled with the waves. Soldiers and sailors littered the deck. The soldiers seemed to get in the way of the sailors as they went about their tasks like a hive of bees working as one. The only thing all the men seemed to have in common was their disapproval of having a woman on board the ship.

"You should confine yourself to below decks," Roger said.

"It's stifling in our cabin," Maretta said as she closed her eyes and enjoyed the sensation of the wind and spray of the sea on her face.

"The captain informed me that your presence unsettles the men, and some have reported strange sounds coming from that infernal box of yours," Roger said as he looked around at the men. He looked paler than she'd ever seen him before. Perhaps the sea air didn't agree with him, or could it be something else, she wondered.

"Darling," Maretta said, ignoring the open hostility from the men staring at her. "It's impossible for any strange noises to emanate from my Kist. They're being hysterical."

"Sailors are a superstitious bunch. Having a woman on board has always been considered bad luck, but now to add that strange box with its engravings to the mix." Roger sighed.

"I knew bringing you was a bad idea. Your place is at home, not on a ship or battlefield."

"But Darling," Maretta said as she tried to scramble for the right thing to say that wouldn't get her beaten and locked in the cabin until they reached the Cape of Good Hope. "You said knowing that I was by your side, even in battle, made our marriage better and stronger than anyone else's. We made a vow never to leave each other's side."

"It was a pretty vow to make at the time, but perhaps it was a foolish one," Roger said as he stepped towards her and grabbed her hand. His eyes flashed with anger. "You should perhaps check on your damned chest and then retire to our cabin now and stay out of the way of these brave men."

"Yes, Dear," Maretta said, pulling her hand out of his tight grip. She wiggled her fingers to regain circulation as she went below deck, away from the men and their open hostility. If a battlefield was dangerous, what was being the only woman trapped on a ship with armed men who seemed to hate women? Perhaps she should have stayed home.

The image of Alistair's face flashed before her as she climbed down the stairs to the hull. The memory of his touch on her hand and his breath on her cheek stirred a longing in her. She couldn't explain her need or the urgency she felt. All she knew was that she had to cross the oceans and face any danger to be with him.

Lanterns swayed with the ebb and flow of the ocean. They barely lit the hull. Shadows reached out of the dark towards the Kist. The goats and chickens kept in the hull to supply the sailors and soldiers with fresh food for the voyage seemed drawn to her box. Some of the goats had escaped their pens and joined the free-roaming chickens around it. A kid was curled up and fast asleep on top of the Kist. She'd never understood the effect it had on animals. Cats especially seemed drawn to it, even when buried.

She heard the whispers emanating from the runes carved into the wood. They were meant to keep the curious away. Only being buried in the ground would silence them. She'd brought a pouch filled with earth to keep them quiet for the journey. Maretta felt a twinge of guilt as she disturbed the sleeping goat and shooed it off the coffin. She then pulled the small bag out of a concealed pocket in her dress and sprinkled some of the sacred earth on the lid. The voices were silenced but would only remain quiet for a short time. She would have to keep sprinkling earth on the top to keep the voices from driving the men on board insane. The sprinkling of sand on the lid would not affect the animals. They would still be drawn to it and its contents.

Her ancestors could only contain and trap Eithne but couldn't undo what Cailleach had done. The animals would always be able to sense her powers. Not even the runes or the nails could keep her power from emitting something they could feel. If she ever awakened, she would have dominion over all animals, storms, and fire. Those abilities had destroyed Maretta's ancestral village and kept her family trapped in fear of what would happen if they didn't keep watch over Eithne for all eternity.

Maretta had grown to hate the burden of it all, no matter how much her mother had tried to claim that the guardianship of Eithne was an honour. It wasn't. It was a millstone around her neck and one she would dearly love to cut herself loose from. But she knew she would only be free from it all in death.

Eithne watched in fascination as the water drained away to the Gods only knew where. Her wet hair smelt of fresh flowers. The water had grown cold, and she shivered as the water pounded against her. Drops of water ran down her body as she stepped out of the shower to escape the cold water.

"You need to turn the water off when you're done," the spirit said. "You can't waste it. It's precious. And next time don't take so long. If you'd hurried up, you wouldn't be so cold now."

Eithne nodded as she tried to rub warmth back into her arms and chest.

"Oh, for heavens ruddy sake," the spirit said as a towel flew through the air and landed on Eithne's head. "Use that to dry yourself off. Bloody half-wit."

"I'm not a half-wit," Eithne said as she rubbed herself with the towel and luxuriated in the feel of the material against her skin. "Cailleach will come and explain this all to me."

"Cailleach isn't coming," the spirit said. "The old Gods are all gone. Now, there's only one God, and he's not exactly the helpful sort. I've always found him to be more of the absent, judgemental father type who doesn't explain a bloody thing."

"That can't be true," Eithne said as she almost reverently rubbed the soft material against her face. "The Gods would never have deserted us."

"Well ..." the spirit said. "We deserted them first, so I can't really blame them for disappearing."

"I don't understand," Eithne said as she dropped the towel.

"That doesn't surprise me. You're not the sharpest tool in the shed."

"What do sharp tools in sheds have to do with anything?"

"As I said. Not too sharp."

A knock on the door interrupted Eithne from asking more questions.

"Are you okay in there," her rescuer called through the door. "I thought I heard voices."

"I'm fine," Eithne said, grateful that her voice didn't falter and hopeful that she'd used the right words in his language.

"Thank fuck you can speak," he said with an audible sigh of relief. "Are you hungry? I can order pizza. Or something else if you'd prefer."

"Whatever you're having is fine with me."

"Okay," he said. "Meat Lover's Pizza okay with you?"

"Anything is fine with me."

"Great," he said with an excited clap.

Eithne waited for the sounds of his retreating footsteps.

"What is pizza?" Eithne asked the spirit.

"It's a type of flatbread with toppings and cooked in a fire oven. It became popular a little after my time, so I've never actually eaten it, but it looks delicious."

"What do you mean after your time? Aren't you from this time? How do you know anything then?" Eithne asked.

She didn't know much about this time, but speaking to ghosts had never been something to advertise, even when Cailleach and the other old Gods had walked the earth. No matter what the century, people intrinsically remained the same. People who were different, who could see the other side, made those who were not and could not uncomfortable. While revered by her people, the Druids were kept at a distance. Witches, though seen as wise women, were often ostracised and feared. Eithne suspected that since the Gods had been replaced and this thing called science had taken the place of magic, speaking to ghosts and being different was not something the people of this time would tolerate any differently. She didn't know the consequences should her rescuer discover who and what she truly was, but she was reluctant to find out.

"You won't get burned at the stake," the spirit said. "They haven't done that in a few hundred years, but they might put you in a state-run asylum, which actually wouldn't be that bad."

Eithne could sense the spirit thinking, and whatever she was thinking, Eithne had a feeling it didn't bode well for her.

8

The cabin was dark and stifling as the ship rocked with each crashing wave. They'd been at sea for almost a month. For most of that time, a storm seemed to follow them, and that storm was growing increasingly worse. There was no fresh air below deck, and the crashing waves made it perilous on deck.

The putrid smell from the bucket she'd emptied her stomach into was not helping either. She contemplated leaving the cabin in search of some tea to settle her stomach and simply get liquid into her weakened body. Another wave sent her reeling back to her bunk and caused another bought of nausea. Thankfully, the bucket was within reach as she retched up the little fluid left in her body. There was also no way of emptying the contents of the bucket. The wind would only send it back. She had known that it would be a difficult journey and that the seas along the coast of Africa were treacherous, but nothing could have prepared her for this.

The cabin door burst open. A soaked Roger stood in the doorway. He held a flickering lantern, illuminating his scowling and dripping wet face. Roger always covered fear with rage. She knew what was coming. She knew that he would use some imagined slight as an excuse. Her mere presence was enough most of the time. Most of the time, she was in a condition to deal with his moods, but at that moment, she didn't know if she had the strength.

"You should have stayed," Roger said as he entered the cabin and quietly closed the door. "The sailors are saying that it's your fault that another of the deckhands was taken by the sea while securing one of the sails."

"That's ridiculous," Maretta said as another wave hit the ship. "It's superstitious nonsense."

"They say we're bound to lose more men in this storm," he said as he hooked the lantern to its chain so that it could sway as the ship rocked instead of flying across the cabin and burning it to ashes.

Maretta wondered if the ship would burn in the storm and which would be the better way to die. Would she prefer drowning, burning, or being beaten to death by her husband? None of the options was particularly appealing.

"If we're lucky, only a few men will lose their lives instead of the ship being wrecked on some reef." Roger took a few more paces towards her.

"I'll pray for the men," Maretta said as she swallowed the little saliva left in her dry mouth.

"Pray to which God?" Roger said as he stood over her, his fists clenched. "The one true God or the ones you think I don't know you secretly believe in and pray to?"

"Roger, please," Maretta said as she tried to sit up. She knew that no matter what she said, it would be wrong. "My family have always been defenders of the faith. You know this."

"I know you come from a long line of witches who should have been burned at the stake," Roger said as he gripped her by the hair and pulled her off the bunk.

She landed on her knees in front of him.

"I can hear her voice inside my head whenever I go below deck," Roger whispered in her ear. "I thought I was going mad until I heard the sailors talking about your Kist and the voice they hear when they're near it. My men are too afraid to go down there and would rather stay on deck and be washed away by the sea." He pulled her hair tighter. "Even the animals in the hold are behaving strangely. They started attacking the men who wanted to throw it overboard. One of the rats plucked a man's eye out. The men also want to throw you overboard with your infernal box. They're calling you a witch. I'm the only thing standing between you and a watery grave." He laughed as he tugged her head back to look up at him. "You should be more grateful that I'm protecting you, my little witch."

"I'm not a witch," she whispered as he let her hair go and unbuckled his belt. He slowly pulled it through the loops. She shuddered as it snapped tight in his grip. She knew her ancestors were watching, but they never intervened. She sometimes wondered if they secretly enjoyed watching her being punished. She came from a long line of cruel and vindictive bastards who only admired power and cruelty in others. Her mother had always admonished her for not being as strong as the rest of her family. She had always been the weak link in the bloodline, and the rest of them, dead and alive, never let her forget it.

Roger was also right about her ancestry; she did come from a long line of witches, but like everything else, she hadn't inherited any powers, only that bloody box. She wished she had inherited just a tiny ounce of Mael Muire's power. Roger would have been the one on his knees. Then, she would have shown them just how strong and cruel she could be.

If only the old Gods were still around and able to grant mortals powers the way Cailleach had done with Eithne, although that hadn't worked out so well for Eithne. Maretta knew she would have been able to do so much more with those gifts, starting with calming the angry sea the sailors wanted to throw her into and which kept dashing her about, making her too sick to deal with Roger's latest need to show her his strength and his flaccid member that only stiffened when he punished her.

In the past, she'd even enjoyed some of the hidings he'd given her. They'd been rather stimulating, but in recent months, his beatings had grown more violent, more enraged. They seemed to have less to do with his insecurities and more with causing her pain and suffering. It was almost as though there was something specific he was punishing her for. As the thought began to take hold, Maretta's heart beat faster, and her mind reeled.

Did he know about Alastair?

Eithne sighed as she considered her reflection in the bathroom mirror. She prodded her face and opened her mouth to look at her teeth. She even wiggled her tongue around. Then, she examined the rest of her body. She cupped her breasts and marvelled at how firm they were. Her stomach and buttocks were also toned. She struggled to come to terms with it being a true reflection of her appearance. She may have looked that good when she'd been a young lass, but as a woman who'd given birth, fought in battles and fallen off her fair share of horses, she'd ceased looking like that long ago. She'd broken bones and been wounded in battle. She'd been murdered and come back from the dead. None of the scars she'd earned in her life were evident on her body. The loss of who she'd been almost made her cry.

"Pizza's here," the Roman called through the door.

"For heaven's sake," the spirit sighed. "You're immortal and attractive. A rather handsome man is also waiting for you on the other side of that door. I can also guarantee that he wants to do things to you. So, could you please stop feeling sorry for yourself and leave this bathroom?"

"What do you mean by 'do things to me'?" Eithne asked, taking a step away from the door. "Does he wish to cause me harm?"

"It's going to be a long afterlife," the spirit sighed again. "He wants to do things that, if I still had the faculty to blush, I would be doing so right now. He wants to mount you, hump you, or whatever you called it two thousand years ago."

"Oh," Eithne said with a smile. "I haven't done that in over two thousand years."

The tears she had kept at bay earlier threatened at the edges of her eyes and stung as she tried to fight the wave of emotions back.

"Please don't cry," the spirit said. "Pull yourself together and get out there and enjoy immortality. Can you do that for both of us since we're trapped together, whether either of us likes it or not?"

Eithne nodded.

"Good," The spirit said, sounding pleased with herself. "Go get 'im."

"Go get what?" Eithne said. "I don't understand."

"Him," the spirit sighed. "Go get him."

"Go get him what?" Eithne asked.

"Oh, for Pete's sake," the spirit sighed again. "Just go."

Eithne left the bathroom feeling even more confused by this new world and how people spoke and expressed themselves than she had thought possible. Nothing in this place made sense. It was exciting, new, and incredibly different from everything she'd left behind, but also overwhelming. A part of her wanted to stay in that bathing chamber, but another part wanted to step outside and explore everything and anything this time and place had to offer.

Walking down the passage towards the sound of plates and cutlery, she reminded herself that she had survived Mael Muire and was immortal. She reminded herself that Cailleach had given her gifts and that she was probably more powerful than even she knew. She nodded to herself with each reminder that she was a powerful woman who could handle anything from the old and the new world.

"Oh!" her Roman said as he looked up from the table where he'd been opening a box of what Eithne assumed was the food. "Did the clothes not fit?"

"The clothes," Eithne said as she tried to think what to tell him. That she'd completely forgotten about them didn't seem an appropriate response. He probably already thought something was wrong with her. She didn't want him to think she was stupid. Having her ghostly companion letting her know that was what she thought of her was bad enough.

"They were a little tight," Eithne finally said. Hoping it was a reasonable excuse.

"Ja," her Roman said as he surveyed every inch of her naked body. "I can see now how that would be the case."

"I can wrap a towel around myself if my nakedness is offensive to you?"

"No," he said. "It's not offensive at all. It's the opposite of offensive."

Eithne smiled as he moved his hands to cover his appreciative bulge.

"You really are gorgeous," he said as he walked towards her. "I know you've been through some serious shit, and you don't have to tell me about it if you don't want to, but I'm one of the good guys, and you can trust me."

He was so close she could smell herbs, leather, and a scent she didn't recognise but reminded her of his metal steed. Her heart beat faster. She hadn't been touched by a man in over two thousand years, and now all she wanted was to feel his hands on her skin and taste him. He licked his lips as she reached out and touched his cheek. Before she knew what had happened, his tongue had found its way inside her mouth and was dancing around her tongue. His hands gripped her arse and pulled her closer. His hard-on rubbed against her.

"Fuck," he groaned as he took a deep breath and rammed his tongue down her throat again.

She wasn't entirely sure how she felt about what he was doing to her. It was so different from how she remembered Giric touching her.

"I don't even know your name," he said, pulling away from her.

"Eithne," she said with a smile. "My name is Eithne."

"Even your name is so different," he said as his fingertips traced circles on her butt cheeks, tickling her. "I'm Nick."

"Hello," she said.

"Hi," he said as his right hand travelled up her spine and ribs to cup her breast while his thumb played with her nipple, sending waves of ecstasy through her body. Giric had never touched her like that. "I've never met anyone like you."

"I've never met anyone like you," she said as she ran her fingers through his short, thick, black hair. Giric's hair had always been long, with a mass of red curls to match his beard. He also always stank of horse shit and sweat. Nick's face was smooth; he smelt clean, almost feminine. He was the absolute opposite of the men she'd known before. Only the Roman legionnaires had short hair and shaved and smelt so fresh. She'd never thought she'd find that appealing in a man, but now she couldn't get enough of his scent and soft skin that was remarkably free of battle scars.

While his thumb continued to play with her nipple, his other hand cupped her quim. He did things to her she hadn't known was possible with his fingers. She laughed as his thumb played with the little nub Giric had always ignored in his hasty attempts to mount and impregnate her. Nick was not in any rush as he teased her body with his gentle and exquisite touch.

"You like that," he whispered in her ear.

"Yes," she sighed as another wave of ecstatic pleasure went through her, making her legs weak. "I want more."

"Help me with my pants, and I'll give you more," he said.

Eithne dropped her hands down to his waist but wasn't sure how to work the contraption holding his pants up.

"You need to unbuckle it," the spirit said. "Don't worry; I'll do it; just give me a little space."

Eithne moved her crotch a few inches away while the spirit made quick work of Nick's buckle and unzipped his jeans. Eithne's hands moved under his shirt and up his chest, enjoying the feel of his muscles and smooth skin.

"Not bad," the spirit said as she pulled his pants down.

"You're amazing," Nick said and then kissed her deeply. His hands once again cupped her bum and picked her up while kicking his feet free of his jeans.

"It's a good thing I'm not alive; otherwise, I would have had a knee in the face and a broken nose," the spirit said as Nick carried Eithne down the passage. "You're welcome, by the way."

The bedroom door slammed shut, and the sound of Eithne's peals of laughter reverberated through Nick's apartment. Eithne had never felt such joy as she experienced in Nick's arms nor felt such pleasure as he thrust in and out of her and played with every part of her body. She never wanted it to end. She sighed with absolute contentment as she drifted to sleep in his arms.

"Enjoy it while it lasts," the spirit said from the dark corner of the room.

9

Maretta lay beaten and bruised on the bunk while Roger snored beside her. He must have exhausted himself whipping her body till she begged him to stop, and he could no longer lift his arm. But even so, she couldn't understand how he could sleep so soundly while the ship bucked and rolled on the stormy sea. Her ripped nightgown lay discarded and bloody in the corner. Every part of her hurt. The only part of her that Roger's belt hadn't struck was her face. He'd even beaten her stomach and breasts while she tried to escape him.

For a brief moment, she considered setting Eithne free and walking onto the deck and into that angry ocean. But if she did that, she would never have a peaceful afterlife. Her ancestors would berate her for the rest of time, and she would be responsible for any havoc Eithne caused. Although for someone trapped in a box and supposedly sleeping like the dead, she managed to create enough mayhem. If she were ever set free, it would be far worse.

Another sailor screamed somewhere on deck as he was pulled into the sea's icy embrace.

She thought of Alistair somewhere on a battlefield in the South African bush. The Boers were fighting using guerrilla tactics, hitting hard and running fast. Roger said it was cowardly, but Maretta thought it was clever. The little correspondence she'd received from Alistair before he went scarily quiet showed a deep respect for the Boer commandos. He'd always believed in respecting his enemy no matter who or how strong they were because they might one day hold his life in their hands.

Unlike Alistair, she couldn't respect Roger. She'd only married him because her parents had forced her. Unlike Alistair, Roger came from a rich and powerful family and would aid in advancing her brothers' careers at court and in the army. Everything was for the advancement of the family and the Clan. She didn't have magic like her mother and grandmother, so she had to be the good, obedient wife to the man they chose for her. If she survived long enough to have a daughter, she hoped her daughter would inherit the magical gifts that had been denied her so she would have more freedom than Maretta had ever had.

She only hoped it would be Alistair's child and not Roger's. The thought of having Roger's seed growing inside her made her want to rip out her womb. It would never be his if she did survive long enough to have a child. Never his, she swore to herself. His bloodline would end with him, no matter what her family wanted.

Roger and his family were even more power-hungry than hers, but his family didn't have the long or magical history that her family could boast. He came from a family of Pirates turned Privateers of the Crown that had bought their way into society with their ill-gotten gains from butchering the local inhabitants across Africa and India, not to mention the slave trade. Their latest endeavours were in the diamond mines of Africa, which was the only reason Roger was going to South

Africa. He wanted to secure his family's assets. He didn't give a damn about Queen and country. Not that she did, either. It wasn't really her Queen or her country.

Roger stirred next to her as the watch bells tolled on deck and another man's final scream mingled with the snapping of wood and rope. She only hoped to survive the voyage and feel dry land beneath her feet. Alistair's face drifted through her mind as sleep finally came for her.

Eithne delighted in the feel of his sheets and his naked skin against her. Her fingers stroked his chest as she kissed his cheek and neck softly.

"Give a guy a chance to recover, Baby," Nick said with a tired grin.

"No," Eithne said as she moved her lips down his body. "I want you all the time."

"Damn, Baby," he sighed. "Look at what you do to me. I can't get enough of you, either."

"Nicky," A woman's voice called from the interior of his flat. "I'm back."

"Fuck," Nick said as he pushed Eithne off him and jumped off the bed. He grabbed his jeans and hopped around on one leg, struggling to put his clothes on.

"Who's here?" Eithne asked.

"I'll explain later, but could you please get dressed," Nick said as he pulled his t-shirt over his head.

"I don't understand," Eithne said as a feeling of disappointment grew in the pit of her stomach.

"I think we both know exactly what's going on," the spirit said from her perch on the edge of the rumpled bed.

"I didn't expect this to happen between us. Please understand," Nick whined as the clip clip of the woman's shoes approached the bedroom door.

"I thought you said I could trust you," Eithne said. "You were one of the good ones, but you're just like my husband and every other disloyal man."

"Wait, you're married?" Nick asked.

"He's dead," Eithne said as the door opened. "I killed him."

"What the fuck," The blond woman shouted as she stepped inside. "Who the fuck is this slut?"

"I can explain everything," Nick said. "It's not what it looks like."

"Oh, really," the blond shouted. "Just like that other bitch the last time wasn't what she seemed."

"Baby," Nick said. "You know I love you. She's just some chick who needed help. She doesn't mean anything to me. I promise. You're the only one for me."

"How fucking stupid do you think I am," she yelled. "I've literally found you with a naked chick in our bed, and the room stinks of sex."

"Baby, please," Nick whined. "I'm sorry. I made a mistake. You know I love you. She means nothing to me. I just picked her up on the road. She threw herself at me. I'm just a weak man. I love you."

"Get that whore out of my bed," the blond screamed.

"Eithne," Nick said. "You're going to have to leave."

"You said I could trust you," Eithne said as she stood on the bed. She felt her anger rising, and with her anger, her power travelled through every fibre of her being. She felt the sparks in her fingertips. "You said you were a good man, but you're just another liar who deserves to be punished."

"Here it comes," the spirit said while still sitting on the edge of the bed.

"Oh my God," the blonde screamed as lightning flew around the room.

Nick ran to his hysterical girlfriend and wrapped his arms around her, trying to protect her as a bolt hit the door, slamming it shut.

"Eithne," Nick shouted over his girlfriend's screams. "I'm sorry. I shouldn't have lied to you. I was only trying to help you. Please stop. I now know how special you are. You don't need to kill us."

"She's a fucking freak," the blonde girlfriend screamed. "You brought a fucking freak into our home. How could you cheat on me with ET?"

"Baby," Nick said. "For once in your life, could you please shut up? I'm trying to save your life."

"If you'd kept your dick in your pants, you wouldn't have to worry about saving my life. How could you fuck that?"

"Baby," Nick said as he tried to inch towards the door while keeping himself between an increasingly angry Eithne and his girlfriend. "We can discuss my broken wing syndrome once we're out of here."

"She is very annoying," Eithne said as she played with the electricity in her hands and drifted a few inches above the bed. "She reminds me of a squealing mouse."

"Eithne," Nick said as he inched a few more steps towards the door with his girlfriend tucked behind him. "I got you away from the people who'd buried you. I saved your life."

"No wonder they buried her," the girlfriend screamed. "You should have left her there."

"Perhaps he *should* have left me there," Eithne said as she drifted closer to the couple. "But he shouldn't have lied to me, and most importantly, you should be silent."

Eithne flicked a bolt across the room, hitting the girlfriend between her eyes. The electricity travelled through her body, and as it travelled, her body began to collapse within itself, shrinking and changing form. Her screams turned into a barely audible squeak. A tiny field mouse scuttled out from under the girlfriend's empty clothes.

"What did you do to Judy?" Nick whispered in disbelief.

"Was that her name," Eithne said. "Perhaps you should be more concerned about what I'm going to do to you."

"I helped you," Nick said. "I was good to you."

"A fact which is the only reason you're still alive," Eithne said as she drifted closer to him and contemplated her options. "But you've also proven to be another faithless man who cannot be trusted."

"Please," Nick begged. "Don't turn me into a mouse."

"I could just kill you and get it over with," Eithne said with a smile.

"Please don't kill me. I don't deserve to die. All I did was not tell you I had a girlfriend. Being a cheater is not worth dying over."

"Really?" Eithne said. "You think you deserve to live."

"Yes," Nick said with conviction.

"But I can never trust you," Eithne said as she inched closer and ran a finger along his face. Tendrils of electric energy touched his skin where her fingers travelled, leaving behind blisters where his skin was cooked.

Nick screamed in pain.

"Please," he begged. "I've learned my lesson. I'll never lie or cheat again. Please don't kill me. I'm begging you."

"You shall live," Eithne said with a smile as more magical power travelled through her fingers and into his body. "But you will be punished."

He screamed as his body began to contract and transform in much the same way as Judy's. A black cat scampered out from Nick's jeans and dashed for a hiding spot under the bed, where he began to hiss.

"Hush now," Eithne said as she crouched and peered under the bed. "I didn't kill you, and I didn't turn you into a mouse. You should be grateful. You're still beautiful."

Nick growled and hissed in response and then started cleaning himself.

10

With the breaking of the dawn came a break in the storm. Ten men were forever lost at sea. The storm had shockingly not blown them off course but had shortened their journey by a few weeks. The Cape of Good Hope was only a matter of days away if the captain's calculations were correct. The astonishing thing was that the ship was barely damaged. The sea had only claimed lives as though they'd been sacrificed to it.

A small voice at the back of Maretta's mind whispered that Cailleach was responsible for the storm. The Hag was also the Goddess of storms. It whispered that the old Gods were not completely gone, and they wanted Eithne on the dark continent for their own reasons. It whispered that Maretta's selfish actions would spell doom for her and all her family. She recognised her grandmother's condescending tone.

Her grandmother had been Eithne's guardian for many decades until she'd become too frail. The Kist had briefly been in her mother's care, but the moment Maretta came of age, it was passed to her. Her mother seemed in a hurry to get it out of her presence, claiming that she had other responsibilities as the clan's matriarch and that Maretta needed to step up and do her duty to the family.

While Roger slept and the crew congratulated themselves on surviving the worst storm any of them had ever seen or that any of their fathers had seen or their fathers before them, Maretta slunk down to the bowels of the ship. Her grandmother's admonitions continued all the way down. She only shut up in the presence of Eithne's remains. Sometimes, Maretta considered spending more time with the box to have a respite from her ancestors. But then she had to listen to the pleading voices emanating from the Kist.

As she made her way down the ladder into the hold, she was surprised by the condition the storm had left it in. If she hadn't known better, she would never have thought the ship had been through a storm. The animals slept peacefully around Eithne's coffin. None of the other cargo appeared to have been disturbed either. She'd expected to wade through a few inches of seawater at least. But not even the ocean or the storm dared disturb Eithne and the creatures surrounding her.

If Cailleach had been responsible for the storm, why hadn't she used it to free Eithne? Or were the old Gods truly gone and powerless? Was her grandmother as paranoid in her afterlife as she had been in life?

"My Lady," a man's voice with a slight Scottish accent that reminded her of the highlands and her childhood, came from the dark shadows. "You shouldn't be down here."

"I'm checking on my cargo," Maretta said as she peered into the gloom, trying to see who had addressed her.

"Your husband will be looking for you," he said as a match lit, illuminating his face as he lit his pipe. His piercing blue eyes and scraggly reddish beard were visible briefly before being swallowed by the shadows. "You should return to your cabin."

"Why are you down here?" Maretta asked, inching closer to the Kist.

"Checking on your cargo," he said, exhaling a puff of smoke. "She appears to remain intact and undisturbed."

"I don't know what you mean," Maretta said as she searched for anything she could use as a weapon.

"Bringing her on this voyage was unwise," he said. Another puff of smoke was exhaled.

"Who are you?" Maretta asked.

"The arrogance of your family is astounding," he said with a sigh. "Do you really think you're the only ones in the entire world who know the story of Eithne's murder and subsequent curse or Mael Muire's lust for power? Your ancestors have a lot to answer for."

"Who are you?" Maretta asked again.

"Tell me something," he said, exhaling another puff of smoke. "Did Eithne really deserve any of what was done to her?"

"I don't know," Maretta said as she looked down at the box. She hated looking at it. "I wasn't there, and honestly, it's not my place to judge any of their actions."

"Do you believe that Eithne was created to be our damnation, or did Cailleach perhaps make her immortal to be our saviour?"

"I think if I fail in my duties and Eithne is resurrected, she will wreak untold mayhem and destruction on the world."

"Do you really believe that, or is that what your family wants you to believe? Have you never questioned what your role in all of this is?"

"We will never know what Cailleach intended, and setting her free on a hope and prayer that a Goddess two thousand years ago created an immortal woman to save us from the Romans is preposterous. Eithne must and will stay exactly where she is."

"I envy you, your certainty. Given your family's crimes over the millennia, I'm not sure I could hold to that conviction."

"Which is why I'm the one charged with keeping watch over Eithne and not you."

"Perhaps," he said with a soft chuckle. "But mark my words. One day, Eithne will be set free, and your family, dead and alive, will be punished for all their crimes."

"I ask you again," Maretta said. "Who are you?"

"Captain," A young soldier called from above.

"Perhaps one day you'll know the greater game you and your family like to dabble in, but for now, duty calls."

Maretta didn't see him move or hear his footsteps moving towards her. One moment, he was somewhere in the shadows of the hull, and the next, he was climbing the ladder behind her. For the first time in her life, her ancestors were deafeningly silent. Their silence was far more frightening than the whispers emanating from the Kist.

Nick mewled under the bed while Eithne paced, trying to get her rage under control. Electricity sparked between her fingers as her unspent power continued to travel through her body.

"You need to learn to control yourself," the spirit said. "You can't turn every man who lies into a cat or every justifiably upset woman into a mouse."

"She called me a freak and said he should have left me to die," Eithne said as a tendril of lightning flashed across the room, hitting the wall and leaving a scorch mark.

"But did she really deserve to be turned into a mouse?" The spirit said as she examined the scorch mark.

"She called me a whore and a freak," Eithne hissed as another flash of lightning hit another wall, shattering a framed photograph of the once-happy couple.

"She had just caught you in bed with her man."

"I didn't even know she existed until she started screaming and insulting me. I didn't deserve to be called a whore. I'm not Mael Muire, who purposely seduced another woman's man."

"Perhaps not, but you did turn her into a mouse."

"But I didn't kill her," Eithne said with her hands on her hips. "I wanted to, but I didn't."

There was a scuffle under the bed, followed by a low guttural growl and a squeak that ended abruptly.

"Looks like that distinction is now mute," the spirit said.

"I still didn't kill her," Eithne said with a smirk. "I'm also not going to shed a tear over her demise."

"Poor woman," the spirit said with a sigh. "Her only sin was loving the wrong man."

"Stop trying to make me feel guilty for what happened to her. What is done is done. I can't undo the past."

"But you can learn from it and maybe not turn anyone else into animals."

"We'll see," Eithne said as she opened and closed bedroom closets, looking for clothes that would fit her.

The spirit sighed while Nick bathed himself, as only a cat with a full stomach could do.

"I want to explore this new world and experience everything it has to offer," Eithne said as she pulled on a pair of Judy's tight jeans, forgetting about the clothes she'd left in the bathroom.

"Great," the spirit said with a sigh. "What could possibly go wrong?"

11

The Cape of Good Hope was a bustling settlement with its five-pointed castle and the flat-topped mountain looming in the distance. It was so unlike London or Edenborough. The heat was stifling. Maretta wished she could remove her corset and roll up her sleeves. The corset didn't help her battered and bruised body. It chaffed against the many wounds Roger had inflicted throughout their voyage.

"Don't dawdle, my love," Roger said as he strode off the gangplank ahead of her. "We need to join the rest of the army under Lord Roberts at the fort for our march up north."

Eithne's coffin was carried by the same cadets who had brought it down the stairs when they left London. They seemed far wearier of the Kist than they had before. The whispers emanating from the box were louder and more insistent than ever before. The young men pretended they didn't hear them, but they weren't doing a good job covering their apprehension or relief when they finally loaded it onto the waiting wagon.

It would take many weeks across perilous territory before they reached Lord Robert's main forces. The train tracks leading up north had been blown up or sabotaged in some form or other by the Boers, so they would be travelling north with wagons, horses and on foot. Only heavier loads like cannons and other emergency supplies would go by train as far as possible and then be loaded onto wagons for the rest of the journey.

A part of her wished she was back in London, but another part of her was excited to be able to explore a new country and experience a completely different way of life. She knew from experience that life on the trail with the army would be difficult and dangerous. It certainly wasn't the sort of life most ladies in her social circle would want. Most were shocked when she told them she would join Roger on the journey. They'd thought marriage would have put an end to the adventures of her youth.

They'd all been shocked when she'd decided to get training as a nurse. She'd wanted to be a doctor, but that vocation was not open to women, regardless of their social status. Her mother still hadn't forgiven her for wanting any kind of career. Women in society did not work. Their only job was to marry well and produce children. Being a nurse was a disgrace to the family name. Her family had declared that she was being eccentric and laughed about it in their friends' and acquaintances' ballrooms and tearooms. She could never tell them the real reason for wanting a profession.

She'd been a qualified nurse who had seen some combat in Sudan when her engagement to Roger was announced. She'd barely known him then, but her family gave her no choice in the match. A part of her suspected her mother's true reason for forcing her to marry Roger and giving her the responsibility of Eithne's care before it was her time. She should have known she couldn't keep any secrets from her ancestors. She thought they'd been so careful. But when you're being spied on by the dead, it doesn't matter how sneaky you think you're being. They always know.

Alistair was shipped off to the Cape colony on the day of her wedding, putting an end to their plans to run away together. She'd managed to get a few letters to him, and he'd managed to write a few, but it took months for any correspondence to reach either of them, which made every word on those few pages of parchment even more special. She'd read every word a few times over and knew them by heart. They were etched into the very fibres of her being.

When she found out Roger would be joining Lord Roberts' and Kitchener's expeditionary forces, replacing General Buller, she'd petitioned Lord Kitchener to join as a field nurse. It hadn't been easy, but in the end, he'd agreed. She could be very persuasive when she wanted something bad enough.

She didn't know where he was stationed or who his commander was. She only knew he was somewhere in this strange country fighting the Boer soldiers. She only knew that she had to find him again, even if it was the last thing she did. He was the only thing in her life that made life worth living. He was the first thing she thought about in the morning and the last thing she thought about at night. He was the only thing she thought about while Roger beat her and forced her to perform her wifely duties. Thinking of Alistair while Roger was inside her was the only thing that gave her any pleasure.

"Darling," Roger said, pulling her away from the image of Alistair naked and smiling. "Are you alright? You look a little flushed."

"Just the heat, my love," Maretta said, looking around and realising they'd arrived at the castle and were surrounded by the British army. She found herself searching their faces, hoping to see his amongst the soldiers standing at attention and waiting to march north. One face she did glimpse was that of the Captain she'd encountered in the hull. He smiled, and then he was gone, swallowed by the crowd.

Eithne's Kist rattled and whispered from the back of the wagon. It was almost as though she was reacting to the Captain's presence. Maretta knew she needed to bury the Kist. Only once Eithne's immortal remains were in the ground would she be quiet. But Maretta would only be able to do that once they reached the Boer capital, Pretoria. She only hoped that Eithne and whatever Gods still lurked in the shadows of this dark continent wouldn't cause too much mayhem on the journey. Then there was the Captain, whoever he was, and whatever his intentions might be, Maretta couldn't trust him. The journey into the interior would be arduous and dangerous, but she had to make it to Pretoria and Alistair.

Eithne wore a pair of Judy's jeans and a black t-shirt while eating a cold pizza slice. Nick sat on the dining room table. His tail swished as he watched her eat. Eithne reached out her hand to scratch his chest, but he swatted her hand away and hissed.

"Is he aware of who he is and what you've done to him?" the spirit asked.

"Yes," Eithne said. "I made sure he knew everything, but he also has the instinct and nature of a cat."

"So, he knows he ate his girlfriend?"

"He does," Eithne said with a smile and picked a piece of meat off the pizza and held it out to Nick, who eyed the morsel for a few seconds before biting into it. Once he'd finished munching it, he licked his jaws and edged closer to the pizza, demanding more meat with his eyes as only a cat could.

"I would have thought he'd be full after eating Sam," the spirit said.

"She was a small mouse with very little meat on her bones," Eithne said. "I don't think she was a filling meal."

Nick meowed.

"You'll get over it," Eithne said as she fed him another piece of meat. "You might even like your new life."

Nick meowed. Eithne reached out and scratched his chest and behind his ears. He let her.

"There you go," Eithne said. "There's no point fighting it."

Nick purred.

"Good boy," Eithne said with a smile as she stroked him.

The spirit floated back and forth as though she were pacing.

"I can feel your disapproval," Eithne said as she pulled another slice out of the box. "Should this be eaten warm?"

"Normally, yes," the spirit said as she floated. "But they also seem to eat it cold the next morning or reheated in the microwave."

"Microwave?" Eithne asked with a mouth full of pizza.

"That metal box on the kitchen counter," the spirit said. "You place your food in it and push a few buttons, and it cooks your food."

"Magic," Eithne said as she examined the microwave and started opening and closing the door and pressing buttons.

"It's not magic," the spirit said. "It's science and technology."

"Just because they've managed to harness the powers of the earth, air, and water and put them in metallic boxes and pipes doesn't make it any less magical."

"Magic no longer matters," the spirit said with a sigh. "Its importance ceased to matter a few hundred years ago. Around the same time, the industrial revolution happened, although the Church had pushed it underground before then anyway. So magic is rather dead."

"No, it's not," Eithne said with a smile. "Magic found another way to thrive. Look around you. It's everywhere. Humans found another way to harness it. It's no longer only available to a handful of druids or old crones. It just has a different name now. It's wonderful!"

Eithne spun around the room while she played with the electromagnetic and sound waves travelling through the air. Nick helped himself to bits of meat on the pizza while the spirit silently watched them.

"Time to go," Eithne said as she suddenly stopped spinning and strode for the door.

"Where do you think you're going?" the spirit said as she tried to block the door.

Nick meowed.

"I'm taking your bike," Eithne said as she touched the door handle, ignoring the spirit. The lock mechanism clicked, and the door opened.

Nick hissed and jumped off the table.

"I'm not going to crash your bike," Eithne said as she headed out with the spirit in tow. The door slammed shut before Nick could escape.

Eithne heard him meowing through the door as she descended the stairs towards freedom and adventure. Her heart beat faster with anticipation as she approached his metal steed that was now hers.

"Do you even know how to ride that thing?" the spirit asked.

"I'm going to figure it out," Eithne said as she stroked the shiny black metallic-painted tank as though it were a lover.

"Are you planning on riding it or seducing it?"

"Both," Eithne said with a grin as she straddled it. "She's going to tell me how she wants me to ride her and how to take care of her."

"It's a machine," the spirit said.

"Don't listen to her," Eithne said as she planted a kiss on the tank. "She doesn't know how special you are."

The engine roared, and Eithne laughed.

"Let's go for a ride," Eithne said as a helmet materialised over her head, and the bike revved her engine before reversing out of her parking spot and taking off down the road towards the estate's main gate and freedom.

"Bugger," the spirit groaned. "I'm going to be in such deep shit."

12

Sweat dribbled down between Maretta's shoulder blades and between her breasts. The arid scenery, peppered with exotic and strangely delicate wildflowers that somehow managed to thrive in the semi-desert of the Karoo, was more beautiful than she had expected. Soldiers marched in formation on either side of the wagon trail, trampling those delicate and wild blooms without thought. A drummer boy kept time on his drum. The constant drumming blended with thousands of boots hitting the ground in unison, lulling her into an uneasy stupor. Flies buzzed around the oxen drawing the wagons. She had to keep rousing herself to swat them away from her face.

She desperately needed to sleep, but when she closed her eyes, she saw visions of Eithne burning the village of her ancestors and screaming when Mael Muire hammered the nails into her body. Maretta felt her rage when she saw Giric marrying a pregnant Mael Muire. She felt the agony of every nail piercing her flesh and when the final nail was hammered through Eithne's heart. It was as though Eithne or something else wanted her to experience everything Eithne had. She woke screaming, and the worried faces of young soldiers stared at her. Her nightmares didn't help the morale of the soldiers who were already on edge marching through a foreign country into battle, with the added strangeness emanating from Eithne's sarcophagus.

Maretta understood that whoever or whatever was behind these dreams or visions wanted her to feel some empathy for Eithne or to at least have some understanding of what she'd been through, but Maretta, like every other member of her family before her, refused to see Eithne as a victim. She may have been one the night Giric killed her, but the moment she rose from the dead and killed all those villagers, she ceased being a victim and became a monster who needed to be contained at all costs.

What confused Maretta was that she'd never had these dreams before. Perhaps it was because she'd never spent this much time near Eithne's Kist and her remains. Eithne had been safely buried in an unmarked grave, and Maretta had never had to spend much time visiting the grave. She'd only ensured the grave remained undiscovered and undisturbed every few weeks. But Eithne had to be guarded, even when buried, so the Kist had to be dug up and brought on the journey to Africa.

Her mother had said it was her responsibility and refused to take charge of Eithne's remains. She'd probably hoped that if she refused, it would force Maretta to see sense and not travel with Roger and the army, but Maretta was just as stubborn as her mother. She knew powerful magic surrounded the coffin, but she hadn't expected that level of torment. She again began to second guess her decision, but then she thought about Alistair, and all doubt disappeared.

"You're scaring the men," Roger said as he rode his horse next to her wagon. "These men have enough to worry about without contending with your witchery."

"Yes, dear," Maretta said. "I will try not to have any more nightmares."

"Female sensibilities have no place in war," Roger said. "If you can't pull yourself together and get control over whatever strange and unnatural things are going on with that box of yours, I will send you and that infernal thing back to England. Do I make myself clear?"

"Yes, dear," Maretta said as Roger galloped away to retake his position at the head of the formation.

Maretta sighed with relief as Roger was swallowed up by the marching sea of red uniforms. One good thing about being on the march was that she hardly saw Roger. When they set up camp in the evenings, she had the wagon all to herself. Roger slept in the command tent with some of the other officers. He felt it would be unseemly if he slept with her. It would give the men the wrong idea and create hard feelings within the rank and file. Maretta didn't argue with his thoughts on the subject. It was the first time in their marriage that she got to enjoy a reprieve from his violent attentions. However, she had her suspicions that it had very little to do with how the soldiers would feel about an officer enjoying the privileges of the marriage bed when their wives were back in England, and more to do with the voices and visions emanating from her Kist.

Maretta needed to get some distance from Eithne. The constant psychic bombardment was draining her resolve, which was probably the whole idea behind the psychic attacks. The forces who wanted Eithne free would whittle away at her until she surrendered. And if she did, all would be lost.

BOUND BY BETRAYAL

Eithne's laughter reverberated inside the helmet as the motorbike roared between her thighs. They sped through the traffic, narrowly avoiding cars. Hooters blasted in their wake. The exhilaration and the freedom the machine gave her were like nothing she'd experienced before. The machine whispered to her as they weaved between the cars. She was finally set free; she gunned her engine to show her pleasure, and then bucked up onto the rear wheel to reiterate how much fun she was having.

Nick had called the machine Jessica after a girl he'd had a crush on in high school. He'd never told Judy that the bike had a name or whom she was named after. It was just another small betrayal in a long line of betrayals ranging in severity. Eithne almost felt sorry for Judy, but then she remembered how the woman had screamed and sworn at her instead of Nick, who had been the guilty party. At least Judy wouldn't have to deal with Nick's philandering ways anymore, and Nick would no longer be able to betray any woman again.

Even though Nick had named her, the machine decided she wanted to keep the name. She liked the name, and Eithne respected her decision. She felt that Jessica had the right to self-determination. Nick had spent years taking care of Jessica and had taken her all over the country. In some ways, he'd been more loyal to Jessica than to Judy. Jessica would miss Nick but understood that Eithne was her new mistress and would enjoy more freedom with Eithne than she had ever had with Nick.

Nick had pretended to be brave around his friends, and when he wanted to pick up some unsuspecting woman, but when it came down to it, he never pushed the boundaries on Jessica. He was always aware of his mortality and feared getting hurt on Jessica. He always rode with fear, but Eithne had no such fear.

Jessica led Eithne on a tour of the city, ending in a warren of restaurants and bars in a neighbourhood called Hazelwood. Expensive sports cars parked on pavements next to bicycles and motorbikes. Parking attendants waved people into tight spaces for tip money. The small neighbourhood had morphed into the city's main dining and drinking hub but didn't have enough parking to cater to the hordes of people exploring the wide variety of food on offer catering to a wide assortment of pallets. Colourful menus written on chalkboards adorned narrow pavements, informing potential patrons of that day's specials. Vegan restaurants nestled next to traditional African eateries cooking chicken and pig's feet on open fires in old houses converted into restaurants and bars.

A bald man with a beer gut whistled as Eithne dismounted Jessica.

"Hey, you sexy thing," he said. "Want a real sex machine between your legs?"

Eithne looked around for this real machine the man spoke of but couldn't see one.

"What machine would that be?" Eithne asked, still looking around for what he could be referring to and feeling confused.

"This one," he said and grabbed his crotch. His friends, who had congregated behind him, guffawed.

Eithne looked him up and down in silence. The man began to fidget while his friends elbowed each other.

"Come sit on my face, and I'll tell you how much you weigh," one of his friends said to a chorus of laughter.

"Why?" Eithne said after a long, drawn-out silence. "Is your nose bigger than your penis?"

"She's got you there," another one of his friends said.

"Fuck you," the man with the big nose said to his friends. "And fuck that bitch. It's her loss."

"Please don't kill them." The spirit said as she leaned against a sports car.

"I wasn't going to do anything to these pigs," Eithne said.

"The crazy bitch is talking to herself," Penis Face said to his increasingly uncomfortable-looking friends.

"You have to admit he's asking for it," Eithne said to the spirit.

"You don't need to rise to the bait," the spirit said. "They're stupid mortal men who don't know any better."

"Perhaps they need a lesson in manners?" Eithne said.

"Who the fuck are you talking to, you crazy bitch?" This time, it was the sex machine who wanted to be heard.

Eithne sighed as she looked at the spirit.

"They're asking for it," Eithne said with a shrug as she turned to face the ego of arseholes. Blue sparks crackled between her fingers.

"You don't need to do this," the spirit said.

"I know I don't have to," Eithne said with a smile. "But I really want to."

Penis Nose squinted and then rubbed his eyes as he noticed the sparks just before one hit him in the face.

"What the fuck?" Was all he managed to say before his nose was turned into a micro-penis.

"That looks to be about the right size," Eithne said.

His hands clamped over what used to be his nose as he tried to figure out what had happened to his face. He screamed as he started to realise what had been done to him.

"Shhhh," Eithne said as his mouth disappeared, and he struggled to breathe. His friends stared at him with confusion as they tried to comprehend what they were seeing.

"What to do with these morons?" Eithne mused. "Calling them pigs or dogs is an insult to those creatures who, unlike these things, are useful and actually quite intelligent."

It only took a few moments for the gaggle of awful men to abandon their suffocating friend and attack Eithne. It only took a few seconds more for two of them to be on the ground with multiple broken bones and internal bleeding. The remainder of their little gang ran off with promises that they would find her later and teach her a lesson she would never forget.

"Happy?" Eithne asked the spirit. "They're still alive."

"That one won't be if you don't let him breathe," the spirit said.

"Fine," Eithne said with a pout as she clicked her fingers, and Penis Face returned to simply looking as though he'd been hit by the ugly stick.

"He'll live," Eithne said. "Although I'm not sure he deserves it. He's not a good man. He's forced himself on more women than I have fingers and toes. But there are worse things than death that will keep you happy and give this vile excuse for a man his just desserts."

Eithne smiled as she sunk down on her haunches next to Penis Face, who was still struggling to regain his breath.

"You've been a very bad man, and you deserve to be punished," Eithne told him.

"Please," he begged. "Let me go. I promise I won't tell anyone."

"Isn't that what countless women said to you just before you violated them?"

"I promise," he said. "I won't hurt another living soul ever again. Please just let me go."

"Don't worry," Eithne said. "I'll let you live, but that pathetic thing between your legs that's bothered you so much for most of your life won't bother you anymore. What no longer exists can't cause any more problems."

He screamed as he felt his favourite toy disappear forever.

Sirens blared in the distance as Eithne climbed back onto Jessica, who revved her engine and sped off.

"That was stupid," the spirit said as she floated beside the speeding motorbike.

"That was fun," Eithne said. "I can't wait to do it again."

13

The encampment at night was eerily quiet. Hushed voices shared past tales of valiant exploits and of families waiting back at home. They spoke with false bravado of what they would do should the enemy attack. The drummer boys had fallen into an exhausted sleep next to campfires while the older boys listened to seasoned soldiers tell their tall tales of adventures in exotic lands.

Maretta strolled towards the officers' tent. She'd been summoned for dinner. Even while trekking across the wild and untamed wilderness and possibly surrounded by enemy soldiers known for their guerrilla tactics and attacking at night, English gentlemen still had to have their luxuries and opulent dinners. Maretta wasn't going to complain about having a proper meal at a well-laid table, but she did find it somewhat ridiculous. She would also have been quite happy sitting around the fire, listening to the rank and file tell their stories while drinking their grog and enjoying their simple stew. She thought of Alistair sitting around a similar fire somewhere further north. Was he telling similar tales to young cadets? Had he told them of his lost love?

As she approached the officers' tent, she tried to put all thoughts of Alistair aside. She took a deep breath, straightened her shoulders, and stepped inside. Candles illuminated the white canvas of the tent. She couldn't help thinking how easy it would be to burn it down with all of them in it.

"Here she is," Roger said with a slight slur. "Isn't she lovely?"

He stumbled over to her and wrapped his arms around her waist.

"I see you gentlemen are already enjoying yourselves," Maretta said as she tried to pry his hands off her.

"Boys will be boys," an officer Maretta hadn't met before said as he raised his wine glass, sloshing red wine.

Roger slithered around her and cupped her breasts from behind.

"Didn't I tell you she has the most amazing breasts?"

They nodded in unison and practically salivated as they watched Roger fondle her. She struggled to find her voice and swallowed the little saliva she had in her mouth. This was not the elegant dinner she had been expecting. These men who pretended to be refined gentlemen in the salons in London had become a pack of rabid dogs, and now they circled their prey.

"What are you doing, Roger?" Maretta whispered.

"Showing off my beautiful and dutiful wife who loves me so much that she followed me into war," Roger said with an edge to his slurred speech.

The tent flap opened behind them. The breeze from the outside caused the candles to flicker.

"Gentleman, is this the usual conduct of the Queen's officers?" A commanding voice said, resulting in a sobering attitude in a few men. The crazed and animalistic haze that had distorted their features only a few moments ago seemed to lift just enough for their judgment to return. Most of them cast their eyes down, unable to meet the disapproving stare from the new arrival.

"This is none of your concern, Captain," Roger hissed as he gripped Maretta tighter and dug his fingers into her breasts. An involuntary whimper escaped from her lips.

"Lieutenant," the new arrival said. "Go patrol the perimeter. That's an order."

Roger snarled as he released Maretta and stormed out of the tent. Maretta crumbled but was caught by the new arrival before her knees hit the ground.

"Thank you," Maretta managed to say as she tried to regain her composure.

"My pleasure," the Captain said as he took a respectful step back.

"I don't know what came over them," Maretta whispered as she turned to face her rescuer.

"Eithne and her curse tend to remove the masks of those around her. She exposes the very worst in those exposed to her for a lengthy period," the Captain said as he crossed his arms.

"How do you know so much about Eithne?" Maretta asked as she recognised the man who had rescued her as the man from the ship. "And who the bloody blazes are you really?"

"I'm just a captain," he said with a smile.

"I somehow doubt that," Maretta said as she crossed her arms.

"I'm not your enemy," the Captain said.

"But you're not my friend either," Maretta said.

"That remains to be seen," he said. "I haven't decided if you're worthy of my friendship. None of your ancestors were, but you're unlike your family."

"Who are you?" Maretta said as she took a step towards him.

The sound of gunfire reverberated outside. The officers, who had slunk off to their cots in confusion and drink-induced stupors, burst into action.

"Finally, we get to see some action," a lieutenant Maretta knew as Ambrose said.

"You should get to the infirmary," the Captain said to Maretta. "Knowing the enemy, it won't take long. They tend to hit fast and hard. The bastards know how to shoot far better than any of these dandies." The Captain gestured at the officers still struggling to get their uniforms on.

"Shouldn't you be rushing into the fray," Maretta said as a bullet tore through the canvas, narrowly missing her head.

"I never rush," he said with a grin.

Another bullet ripped through the canvas and hit Ambrose in his shoulder. His face was confused and surprised as blood seeped through his white shirt. Maretta sprang into action. All her fear was pushed aside as her medical training kicked in.

The Captain laughed as he ducked out of the tent and strolled into the night as bullets flew and panicked men and boys shouted or cried. Maretta heard him barking orders at the men, restoring some semblance of order to the chaos of battle. Veteran soldiers flocked to his side. Burning torches were flung onto tents, setting them alight, including the Officers' tent. Maretta managed to drag Ambrose out as it began to smoulder.

Just as suddenly as it had begun, it was over. The Boer soldiers disappeared as silently as they had attacked. A hyena laughed in the dark. The burning tents and supplies illuminated the eyes of the pack of wild beasts. Maretta couldn't help but feel that even the animals in this strange land were watching and waiting to attack. She felt surrounded. Ambrose whimpered as she inspected his wound. Unlike one of the young boys who had been listening so avidly to the fireside tales of war just a few hours before, he would live.

The infirmary had been one of the tents that flames had engulfed. The wounded and dying lay in haphazard rows on the uneven ground. A lion roared in the distance, probably attracted by the smell of fresh blood. Doctors and nurses were visibly shaken by the realities of war but managed to focus on the job at hand and those who could be saved. Those who couldn't were made comfortable.

Maretta helped Ambrose find a space amongst the rest of the wounded. She searched their faces for a glimpse of Roger and the Captain but didn't see either. She also found herself searching for Alistair; even though she knew he wouldn't be there, she couldn't help herself. The closer she got to where he'd last written to her from, the more it felt as though her heart had a dagger in it. All she wanted to do was cry or shout or scream. It took everything she had to keep her composure. She could feel those ropes she'd tied around herself so tightly beginning to fray.

"I see you survived your first skirmish with the enemy relatively unscathed," the Captain said.

She hadn't seen or heard his approach and had to restrain her natural impulse to flee but instead focused on tending Ambrose's wounds before moving on to another wounded soldier.

"Are you always so quiet?" Maretta asked as she tried to calm herself and slow her breathing down while she cleaned and stitched a head wound that was bleeding profusely.

"We'll be crossing the Orange River near Hope Town soon. Lord Roberts isn't sure what we'll find when we get there. We're hoping the bridge is still intact. If not, we'll be swimming across."

"Why are you telling me this?" Maretta said as she bandaged the soldier's head and moved on to the next one.

"Just enquiring after your well-being," the Captain said.

"I didn't hear an actual enquiry into my well-being in that," Maretta said. "But as you can see, I'm fine, unlike these poor souls."

"These poor souls are in good hands," the Captain said. "And speaking of poor souls, have you ensured that a certain other soul in your care is still intact after that little skirmish?"

"I've been a little busy," Maretta said, trying to restrain herself from slapping the smug look off his face.

"I'm sure this young cadet is fine, and you can be spared for a few moments while you check on our friend."

"Fine," Maretta said as she washed her hands in a bowl of water that had already been stained red by the blood of soldiers washed off the hands of the doctors and nurses.

She swore at the Captain under her breath as she walked through the bullet-strewn, blood-drenched and burned camp. Monkeys chattered in the trees as she approached her wagon, which was thankfully still intact. A shadowy figure moved inside the wagon while a hyena laughed at her again.

The hair at the nape of her neck prickled, and her heart rate jumped. Something was off. No one should have been in her wagon, and the hyena wouldn't stop laughing. As she got closer, cold perspiration dribbled down her already tingling spine. When her hand touched the wagon, everything was silent. The monkeys stopped chattering, and even the hyena was quiet. Even the air seemed to stop moving. Not a single leaf stirred. Only the shadow moved inside the wagon. She tried to climb up but felt frozen in time. Her breath came in ragged gasps.

"Don't move," the Captain said from behind her.

"I can't move," she whispered.

A roar erupted from inside the wagon. She wanted to run but couldn't. Blood pounded in her ears, and her stomach felt as though it was no longer attached to the rest of her body. The Captain edged past her and slowly parted the canvas of her wagon. A lioness with the remains of a fresh kill reclined on top of the Kist.

"Cats," the Captain said with a grin and shook his head. "No matter how big they are, they're no different from their domestic cousins and bring treats for their humans."

Before Maretta could respond to what he'd said or exhale the breath she'd been holding, the Captain jumped inside and started petting the lioness, who seemed to enjoy the attention. Maretta couldn't believe her ears when she heard the enormous cat purring or the things the Captain uttered while he stroked and scratched the lioness's head.

"Who's a good girl?" the Captain said as the big cat nuzzled his hand. "It's certainly not that human who's supposed to be keeping Eithne safe, now, is it?"

"What is that supposed to mean?" Maretta screeched. "Eithne is fine. She's still in her box. She hasn't been freed. What's your problem?"

"Anyone of these soldiers or the monkeys in the trees around this wagon could have climbed in here while you were running around and freed her without even knowing what or why they were doing it. They would feel the compulsion to pry the coffin open and dig those nails out of her remains. Or what if one of the Boers had flung a burning torch on your wagon, turning her bones to ash? And what if one of those bullets from last night had hit you? What if you'd been killed in action? Who would then take charge of her? Who would take her back to England? You have no heir."

"Why do you care what happens to her?" Maretta asked. "And honestly, I thought you wanted her to be free."

"I do," the Captain said. "But not here and not now."

"I don't understand," Maretta said.

"I don't expect you or any member of your meddling family to understand things beyond your pedestrian ambitions."

Before Maretta could respond, he was gone, leaving the sleeping lioness behind and Maretta more confused than ever.

"Who the hell is he?" Maretta asked the lioness, who stretched out even more on top of the Kist.

Eithne and Jessica screeched to a halt at a red traffic light at a busy intersection. Hawkers offered hats, sunglasses, and children's toys to drivers who closed their windows at their approach. A woman in a white Mercedes SLK repeatedly shook her head as she stared straight ahead, ignoring the frustrated hawker peddling cheap goods to feed his family. The light changed, and the woman sped away, almost knocking over the hawker who dropped some of his goods as he jumped out of the way. Eithne narrowly missed riding over his wares, but the driver behind her didn't.

As she rode away from the angry hawker cursing the rich, Eithne felt the pull of ancient and powerful magic coming from the heart of the city. It called to her. It was as though whoever was behind the voice had been waiting for her.

"Don't go," the spirit said. "Nothing good will come from this."

"I have to know," Eithne said as she accelerated away from the suburbs and into the city, passing the Union Buildings and Embassies.

The atmosphere changed the closer she got to her destination. Derelict apartment buildings with washing hanging from windows replaced suburban homes with high walls and tidy gardens. The sun played peek-a-boo behind high-rises. Then, the high-rises were replaced by buildings that had stood for hundreds of years since the city's inception and museums that the city's inhabitants seemed to have forgotten existed. The Natural History Museum was on one side of the street, and The City Hall was on the other. Pigeons nested on statues of long-dead men who had fought for their freedom only to subjugate others.

But the presence that called to her wasn't in either of those buildings. Eithne stopped Jessica in front of a store hidden in the shadows. The services provided were spray-painted on the glass in bold red letters. Everything from removing curses to curing sexual issues to financial services was offered. Even though Eithne had never learned to read anything besides the runes, she knew what the words said. She felt the power emanating from within. Whoever was inside the shop was ancient. Even older than Eithne. And they had more power than she could have imagined, possibly even more powerful than the great mother, Cailleach.

There were others on the streets watching her. They were mortals who served the one inside. They considered themselves dangerous men, but Eithne could swat them like the flies they were if she felt like it. Only the voice from inside kept her from spraying their blood across the walls and pavements as they had done to others who had strayed across their path.

"Don't go in there, please," the spirit begged.

"What don't you want me to know?" Eithne asked as she walked towards the shop entrance.

The spirit didn't answer.

The door opened before Eithne could press the buzzer—the shop smelt of herbs and spices with a tinge of decay.

"Welcome, Sister," a girlish voice said from deep shadows at the back of the store. The voice didn't match the power Eithne felt emanating from the being behind it. She knew it wasn't human but didn't know what it was. She had her suspicions but couldn't be sure.

"Why do you call me sister and yet hide yourself," Eithne said as she tried to peer into the depths of the shadows.

A giggle bounced off the walls. Eithne sighed. She decided that trying to see through whatever masking and shielding spells had been cast was a waste of time, so she wandered the shop and inspected the strange trinkets and spell-casting ingredients on the shelves. The more interesting and powerful items would not be lying in the open but probably hidden at the back of the shop, currently cloaked in darkness. Eithne tried reaching out with her senses to get through the entity's cloaking spells but couldn't penetrate her defences. The only information she could get was that it was female, ancient, and meant her no harm. Eithne also felt that whoever she was, she was bored and lonely.

"You won't be able to see anything I don't want you to see," the girlish voice said. "I've been doing this longer than you've been asleep."

"You invited me here for a reason," Eithne said. "Please show yourself so we can talk and get to know each other. Maybe we can be friends."

Mirthless laughter reverberated through the shop, but it was no longer the giggle of a little girl. The laughter was not that of a child or a teenager but a young woman. Shadows moved and took form. An elegant bare foot emerged, and then a leg. A girl of about eighteen slowly showed herself and stepped into the light. Shells and bones were woven into her braids that cascaded down her naked back. Her eyes were like a lioness on the prowl. Her smile revealed two rows of sharpened teeth. Her canines would have made any lion or tiger jealous. As she strolled towards her, Eithne almost expected her to morph into a lioness. There was something familiar about her. Eithne couldn't shake the feeling that she knew her, even though that was impossible.

"I've been waiting for you for so long," the girl said as she stood in front of Eithne, reaching to touch her arm. "But I see you haven't quite escaped your jailer."

"Don't listen to her," the spirit said.

"Maretta," the girl said. "I see you haven't learnt anything during your time in the spirit realm. You didn't have any power when you were alive, and you certainly don't have any now."

"I kept you away from her for over a century," the spirit said with a petulant tone.

"I was never meant to free her, only protect her. That honour was always meant for someone else," the girl said.

"Do you mean to say that those two children were always meant to dig her up?"

"I don't know," the girl said. "All I know for sure is that she was resurrected at exactly the right moment."

"Who are you?" Eithne asked.

"Are you asking me or your jailor?" the girl asked, glancing at the diaphanous form floating behind Eithne.

"I want to know who you both are and how you know each other, but let's start with the living," Eithne said, crossing her arms and stepping away from the girl. "Who are you, and why do I feel we've met before?"

"Because we have," the girl said. "Well ... Not exactly. You were in a box at the time, and I was in my cat form, but I kept you safe on your journey through this country."

"She was perfectly safe without your interference, Thandi," the spirit the girl had called Maretta said.

"And you're a descendant of Mael Muire," Eithne said as she spun around to face Maretta. "I dare you to deny it."

"I don't deny it," Maretta said. "I'm just as cursed by my family as you are."

"I somehow doubt that," Eithne said.

"I'm trapped here on this plane of existence to watch over an immortal that my overly ambitious ancestors created, and because I was murdered before I could birth a daughter to take over my guarding duties, my grandmother punished me by making you my problem for all eternity," Maretta said. If she'd still been alive, she would have sobbed.

"Wow," Thandi said. "Almost two hundred years, and you're still filled with self-pity. I would suggest therapy, but I don't know any therapists who specialise in ghosts and would have the patience to deal with you. If you're interested, I know a few exorcists who can put you out of your misery."

"That was uncalled for," Maretta said.

"Enough," Eithne shouted, causing the contents on the shelves to shake. "Firstly, your ancestors did not create me. The mother Goddess, Cailleach, did. Your ancestors cursed me and prevented whatever Cailleach's plans for me were. And now I'll probably never know why she resurrected me in the first place or why I've been awoken now."

"That might not be completely accurate," Thandi said with a grin.

"You can't," Maretta said. "I won't let you do this."

"How are you going to stop me from showing her the way?" Thandi said. "In case you haven't noticed, there are no iron nails for you to throw at her, and you sure as shit won't find a cursed sarcophagus that you can bury her in here."

“I will find a way to stop you from unleashing her onto the world,” Maretta said but didn’t sound very sure of herself.

“I’m not unleashing her on anything,” Thandi said. “She isn’t totally good or completely evil, but she does deserve the answers your ancestors prevented her from getting, and I will help her get them. What you do is up to you. You can keep trying to please your long-dead and evil family, who deserved their bloody ends, or you can finally figure shit out for yourself for a change.”

“I can’t allow Mael Muire and her descendants to stop me anymore,” Eithne said to Thandi. “Please help me.”

“Come with me,” Thandi said, taking hold of Eithne’s hand and leading her towards a door at the back of the room shrouded in darkness until Thandi took Eithne’s hand.

“This is such a bad idea,” Maretta said as she followed them through the door.

14

The Lioness was still stretched out and fast asleep on top of Eithne's Kist as Maretta watched the sunrise. The vibrant reds and oranges were so different to the last sunrise she'd seen in London. The sounds of soldiers breaking camp and orders being barked were hushed by the early morning mist, which was more ethereal and otherworldly than the London fog she was used to. It was like the mist of Scotland's highlands and her childhood running wild in the glens. The big cat snored loudly, utterly unperturbed by the humans around her.

"She does sleep soundly, doesn't she?" the Captain said, inches behind her.

"Where the devil did you come from?" Maretta asked, struggling to keep her composure and not betray how much he'd startled her.

"I try to be where I'm least expected," he said with a grin. "She won't take kindly to being disturbed. If I were you, I'd leave her be. She'll leave when she's hungry or gets bored."

"You speak as though you know her," Maretta said.

"We've crossed paths before," the Captain said as he stroked his beard. "She has a rather volatile nature, even for a cat, but once she considers you a friend, she's more loyal than any well-trained canine."

"Would you say that she considers you a friend?" Maretta asked with a smirk.

"I don't think she's quite made up her mind yet, but considering I still have all my limbs, it's looking positive." He smiled as he climbed up and scratched the lioness's head and behind her ears. She rolled her head so he could scratch her chin as well.

"I think I prefer you in your cat form," the Captain said with a chuckle.

The lioness opened her eyes, swatted his hand away with one of her large paws, stretched and went back to sleep. The Captain laughed as he climbed back down and walked past Maretta.

"Where do you think you're going?" Maretta called after him.

"I have soldiers to get in line and across a river. Dealing with stubborn women is not my forte," he said with a wave and disappeared into the throng of soldiers packing up the camp.

Maretta sighed as she glanced at the lioness stretched out on the Kist. She couldn't help feeling like the large cat was watching her through her closed eyelids. She also couldn't quite shake the feeling that she was being judged.

"Fine," Maretta said. "Stay there. If one of the soldiers shoots you, it's not my problem."

The lioness made herself more comfortable in response, while Maretta sighed as she pulled the wagon's canvas together and tied it, trying to hide the Kist and the large cat from prying eyes as best she could. She spotted Roger coming towards her just as she finished tying the ropes to get underway.

"Bugger," she swore under her breath. She was tempted to untie the ropes and climb in the back with the lioness. If only the train tracks north hadn't been blown up, she could have avoided all of this nonsense, but then she would also have run the risk of being unable to find Alistair.

"Where the bloody blazes have you been," Roger shouted. His speech was slurred, and he was still drunk from how he stumbled across the uneven terrain. How he'd survived the night was a mystery and, if she was honest, a little disappointing. Some of her wished he'd made himself an easy target for one of the Boer snipers. His red officer's coat should have made it easy enough for them.

"I was tending to the wounded," Maretta said as she made her way to the front of the wagon and her oxen to ensure their harnesses were secure and remove their feeding bags.

"Lying bitch," he shouted as he grabbed her by the shoulders and spun her around, twisting her ankle. "I know you weren't at the infirmary the entire night. I saw you leave with that trumped-up bastard."

"You were too drunk to see straight last night, let alone see me go off into the wilderness with a strange man," Maretta said as she tried to wriggle out of his grip.

"I know what I saw, Maretta," Roger hissed into her face and tightened his grip.

"You're still three sheets to the wind, and you stink of grog and cigarettes," Maretta said as she tried to distance her face from his breath.

He loosened his grip on her shoulders just long enough to punch her in the gut. She slumped to the ground in a puddle at his feet. Roger yanked her back up to her feet and shook her.

"I am your lord and master," Roger shouted. Spittle sprayed her face. "You will speak to me with respect. Is that in any way unclear?"

Maretta didn't have a chance to respond or regain her breath or any semblance of coherent thought when the lioness bolted from the back of the wagon with a fire-breathing roar that almost set the wagon on fire.

Roger released Maretta and slowly turned towards the fire-breathing lioness, his face turning ever paler. His trousers developed a tell-tale wet patch at his crotch. Maretta wasn't sure how to react to any of what was happening. It all seemed to happen in slow motion. The lioness looked from Roger to Maretta and then back at Roger. Her eyes seemed to penetrate through all their layers to their very souls. Maretta couldn't shake the feeling that she was once again being weighed and measured and that Roger, too, was being judged and found wanting. The lioness's stance changed, and her muscles tensed in preparation to pounce. Roger ran. The lioness made a mock charge but seemed to get bored mid-stride.

Maretta was frozen in place as she watched the cat transform into a girl on the verge of blooming into womanhood with bones woven into her braids. She seemed completely unphased by her nakedness as she sauntered off into the veld, leaving Maretta alone and in shock. She'd always known there was magic in the world but had never seen such a display of raw power. She wasn't sure if she was petrified or excited by the revelation. She also couldn't shake the feeling that she'd see the young woman again. She just wasn't sure whether she would be in her cat form or as a human. Maretta also wasn't sure if she could be trusted. Only time would tell if this magical being was friend or foe.

Wind howled around them as they stepped over the threshold and into a different place and time. The hills of Eithne's childhood rose around them as the door disappeared behind them. A hermit's cottage stood in its place. Sheep bleated in the valley below.

"I know this place," Eithne said as she looked around. "My father's village is not far from here, but I was never allowed to come here as a child. Only my father and a few village elders would come here with offerings in bad times, but he never spoke of whom he came to see. It was only ever talked of in whispers."

"This is a sacred place," Thandi said, smiling at the cottage. "There was a time when humans would come here and ask for favours. They'd come from far away and bring their best sheep or whatever they had as offerings. Sometimes, they even brought their children if they had nothing else to sacrifice. It's nothing like my temple, where people used to worship me, but it's still quite charming. To each their own, I guess."

"I can't be here," Maretta said. "I want to leave." Her voice rose to a high pitch. "Why can't I leave?"

"Well ... there is the whole being tied to Eithne thing, so that could be why, but he probably also doesn't want you to," Thandi said.

"No. No. No. No," Maretta said as she tried to step away from the cottage. "This can't be happening."

"What's wrong with her?" Eithne asked.

"I've given up trying to figure her out," Thandi said. "But you need answers, and she needs to deal with her shit. Plus, this should be interesting, and I might enjoy this a little too much, but I have to take my amusement where I can these days."

The cottage door opened, and a man in a kilt and white shirt stood in the doorframe. He wasn't what Eithne had been expecting. He certainly wasn't dressed in deer skins like the men of her time.

"You fucking bastard!" Maretta screeched.

"Do you know each other?" Eithne asked a fuming Maretta.

"He's the reason I'm dead," Maretta said.

"That's not entirely accurate," the man said.

"Well," Thandi said. "To be fair, you were always going to end up dead. What happened to you was out of his control."

"Don't," Maretta said. "You're just as much to blame for what happened to me as he is."

"And that has always been your problem, Maretta," Thandi said. "You still can't take responsibility for your own choices."

"So this is Eithne?" He asked, interrupting their bickering. "She's finally awake after all this time."

Thandi nodded with a grin as the man strode towards Eithne and cupped her face.

"She looks younger than I thought she'd be," he said as he scrutinised her face.

"Don't we all," Thandi said. "I look eighteen, and I'm older than you."

"Good point."

"Could someone explain what's going on and who this man is who thinks grabbing my face is perfectly acceptable behaviour during a first encounter?" Eithne said as she pulled his hands away from her face.

"Says the woman who slept with the man who picked her up on the side of the road within an hour of meeting him," Maretta said.

"That was an entirely different situation," Eithne said.

"I'm just saying that you didn't have a problem with strange men touching you a few hours ago."

"Could you stop," Thandi said to Maretta.

"Let me introduce myself," he said. "I am Taranis."

Eithne gasped as she fell to her knees.

"Please forgive me," Eithne said with her eyes downcast.

"Oh, for heaven's ruddy sake," Maretta said. "Get up."

"I forgot what it's like to have people kneel at my feet," he said.

"I miss it," Thandi said.

"You could always return to using your old name," he said.

"Maybe, but it also gets tedious after a while. All that bowing and scraping and dealing with all their demands. Humans are so needy."

"I know. They really are annoying," he said, reaching down and pulling Eithne to her feet. "That's why I get so much pleasure from hitting the occasional human with a thunderbolt. It's one of the few pleasures left to me."

"I miss the days when I could stalk the African savannas without being trapped by fences. However, I do enjoy ripping apart the odd poacher now and then. I prefer hunting hunters. It's more sporting, don't you think?"

"We get it," Maretta said. "You're bored. Can we please move on to why you brought us here?"

"I brought her here," Thandi said. "You, unfortunately, have to go where she goes."

"Enough!" Eithne said. "You brought me here for answers, not to bicker with a dead woman."

Thandi shrugged, Maretta sighed, and Taranis smiled.

"Where is Cailleach?" Eithne asked.

"Honestly," Taranis said. "I don't know. I haven't seen my sister since she made you immortal. None of us have seen her or heard of anyone else seeing her. You are the last person to have seen her."

"Do you know why she made me immortal or gave me these powers? Do you know what my purpose is?"

"Does anyone truly know their purpose for being?" Taranis said with a shrug.

"Then what was the point of bringing me here?"

"I might not have all the answers you're looking for or hoping for, but I know that Cailleach wouldn't have brought you back from the dead just for shits and giggles. She always had a reason for doing everything. My sister was all about creating balance."

"How was making Eithne immortal going to create any kind of balance?" Maretta said. "She's the exact opposite of balanced."

"That can be laid at your family's feet," Taranis said. "If Mael Muire hadn't interfered, our lands would have been better protected from the Roman invasion and that pesky religion that came in its wake. Magic and the old ways would have had a champion."

"I thought you didn't know why I was created," Eithne said.

"I don't," Taranis said. "Not for sure, but I have my suspicions. I think she knew what was coming and hoped you'd be a warrior for our kind. We underestimated what that little upstart and his church would do to us and the violence that would come with his zealots. Mael Muire's actions set off a chain reaction that rippled through time and set the world on a different path."

"And we ended up scattered and lost," Thandi said.

"Oh, please," Maretta said. "You're powerful immortal beings. You're not weak, little victims. Spare me the pity party. You could have stood together but chose to fade into the background and be forgotten. You even changed your name, Thandi. You don't get to lay the blame just at Mael Muire's feet. She was just an ambitious mortal who knew a few magic tricks."

Taranis and Thandi laughed.

"Is that what you really believe?" Taranis said. "That Mael Muire was some witch who knew a bit of magic?"

"Yes," Maretta said as she crossed her arms.

Taranis and Thandi laughed again.

"You have so much to learn about your family, you poor stupid human," Thandi said as she and Taranis led Eithne and Maretta inside the cottage.

15

Maretta enjoyed the feeling of the sun's warm caress on her skin as the oxen lumbered in front of her wagon and the flies buzzed around them. She hadn't seen Rodger since the incident with the lioness two days ago and many blissfully quiet kilometres through the African bush. She also hadn't had to endure the Captain's annoyingly enigmatic company. Sometimes, she caught herself wondering what he was up to, but those thoughts were fleeting. She knew he and Roger were with Lord Roberts, beating the Boer army into retreat, and only heard the occasional shots being fired during the skirmishes.

She had spent her days in her wagon with just the whispers from the Kist for company while soldiers marched ahead of her and the rest of the wagon train. Her nights were spent patching up wounded soldiers in the infirmary. She knew the peace and quiet wouldn't last. The further north they went, the closer to the Boer strongholds they got and the more likely it was that the fighting would get more heated and would spread to the wagons and the support staff that usually accompanied an army on the move.

The Orange River was only a few kilometres away, and once they crossed the bridge, they would be entering the Boer Republic of the Orange Free State. She'd heard from one of the other nurses in the infirmary that they would camp at Hope Town to gather supplies before crossing the bridge. The officers would probably commandeer one of the local establishments for their stay. While she longed for a taste of civilisation, a proper bed, and maybe even a hot bath, the thought of having to stay in a room at an inn filled her with dread. It meant having to be in the same room with Roger for appearance's sake.

Roger would not have spent their time apart on internal reflection. Instead, those moments would have been consumed by the gnawing compulsion to incessantly pick at his bruised ego like a festering wound. The slightest pressure would cause it to burst, probably all over her. The thought made her want to scream. She was torn between her desire to escape and a more violent reaction to the injustice of her situation. The idea of smothering him in his sleep or using his belt on him almost made her smile, but then the thought of the hangman's noose made the smile dissolve from her face like a fragile whisper carried away by the wind.

She smelt the town before she saw it: the odour of scorched wood and lingering gunpowder, a sharp reminder of the ongoing war. The air seemed to crackle with tension, mingled with the faintest traces of despair. Hope Town appeared to be a misnomer for the wreck they rode into.

Pale, gaunt and starving faces stared back at her through dirty, broken windowpanes as she rode through the town. She doubted the army would find provisions or an inn to spend the night. The latter was almost a relief, but one she instantly felt guilty over. The people who called this town home had been caught up in a conflict they had no say in. Their homes and livelihoods had been destroyed over the idea of freedom, but what was freedom if your home and crops were set on fire?

In the heart of what seemed to be the town square, soldiers lingered, suspended in anticipation of orders, as the townsfolk hurriedly closed shutters and emphatically slammed doors. Persistent flies swirled around grim pools of blood in the streets, where Maretta imagined the freshly dead had been lying only recently. Hostility permeated the air. It cast its shadow over the town, and everyone still breathing.

Roger's angry shouting drifted over the sound of flies buzzing and the hushed, nervous voices of the soldiers. It was strange how the constant whispers from Eithne's box seemed quiet once she'd entered the town. She couldn't help but wonder if the Kist knew something she didn't. If only Roger would follow its example and stop his yelling. It took her a few moments to understand what he was on about or that he was shouting at her for no other reason than that of still being on her wagon and not being at some empty house they'd been billeted in. How he expected her to know that she was supposed to go to some unknown house instead of following the rest of the wagons was a mystery to her.

"Are you deaf and dumb?" Roger shouted again.

"I'm sorry, Darling," Maretta said in an attempt to defuse the very public scene he was making. He would take it out on her even more severely if she argued with him in front of witnesses, especially men under his command. She needed to be able to sit for the rest of their journey north, which would still take a few weeks or even months, depending on the resistance from the Boers. "I must have gotten turned around. You know I have a terrible sense of direction."

"You don't just have a terrible sense of direction," Roger said as he climbed onto her wagon. "You have no sense at all. Now move over and give me the reins. I'll ensure you get to where you're supposed to be without getting distracted."

"Of course, my love," Maretta said as she swallowed any hope of avoiding a beating. She knew what awaited her the moment they were alone, and from the pitying looks from the soldiers watching her, so did all the men, but none of them would do anything to stop it.

The house wasn't far from the square. Fresh blood puddled on the once-white wooden steps leading up to the front door. Bullet holes pock-marked the walls.

"What happened here," Maretta asked as she tried not to step in any of the blood.

"The people here were trading with the Boers and not loyal to the crown," Roger said as he grabbed her arm and pulled her towards the door.

"Do you mean to say that we did this to them?" Maretta asked as she wrenched her arm free of his grip.

"We can't have Boer sympathisers at our back when we cross the river," Roger said as he grabbed her again, his fingers digging into her flesh.

"Did Lord Roberts give the order for this? I can't imagine him doing this."

"Lord Roberts and that priggish Captain of yours are scouting the bridge. They left me to do the dirty work of securing our rear. Now, stop asking questions about things that don't concern you. You will do as you're told. Do you understand me?"

Maretta nodded. Further questions would only provoke him further, and looking at the blood that had been shed on his orders, she began to wonder what he was really capable of. Had she underestimated just how violent he could be?

He let go of her with a quick, easy smile that hinted at his pleasure as his fist smashed into her stomach, forcing her to crumble to the dusty road. Her hands splashed into the puddle of blood. He grabbed her by the hair, igniting a surge of fear and anger inside her. She could smell the gunpowder from the spent cartridges littered across the wooden floor as he dragged her, kicking and screaming inside the confines of the house. She didn't care who heard her screaming anymore. To hell with decorum and societal niceties. She needed someone at long last to hear her. Even if they did nothing, she needed someone to know what was happening to her.

If only the Lioness hadn't turned into a girl and sauntered into the bush. She could do with a fire-breathing demoness or witch to rescue her. A part of her wanted to find the strength to save herself, but fear of what Roger would do if she fought back stayed her hands.

"Shut your mouth, woman," Roger said. "Or I'll shut it permanently."

"Please, Roger," Maretta begged. "I haven't done anything to deserve this."

"Shut your lying, whore mouth," Roger said as he let go of her hair long enough to slap her. "I know all about your lover, Alistair. He's the real reason you've come all this way. It wasn't for the love of me or our marriage or any of the lies you've told to manipulate me. And now to see you carrying on with that self-important peacock of a man. A witch will not cuckold me." His fists clenched and unclenched as he struggled with his rage.

"I haven't seen Alistair since I was a child," Maretta said as she tried to stem the tides of her own rage. She knew she needed to defuse the situation; the only way to do that was to lie. She needed to lie more convincingly than she had ever done before. Her life depended on it.

"My love," she said as she struggled to her knees in front of Roger, whose breaths came in gasps. "You are the only man I have ever been with. You know this. I was a virgin when I came to our marriage bed. You saw and felt the evidence of that yourself on our first night together. No magic can fake that. And as for the Captain, I have no interest in the man. He may have designs on me, but I do not pretend to know what those are. I only want to be a good wife to you."

Her blood-stained hands reached out to his dirt and blood-encrusted boots. Her fingers slowly moved up his legs.

"Please, my love," Maretta whispered. "Let me be a good wife to you."

"Oh, you are good," Roger whispered, gripping her hair again and yanking her head back. "But I've seen through all your lies now. I know you for the wicked temptress that you are. I've seen you cavorting with demons. I will beat the witchery out of you if it's the last thing I do."

"I didn't summon her. I'm not even sure what she is," Maretta said as she struggled against his grip. If he'd merely thought she was being unfaithful, that would have been something she could have convinced him of her innocence of, but summoning demons, especially when he'd seen her in the presence of a fire-breathing lioness, was a whole other problem.

Bridget Cleary had been beaten and burned by her husband for being a witch just a few years ago, and even though he'd been sentenced to twenty years in prison, his wife was still very much dead, and Maretta didn't want to join her. Roger's family would get him out of any trouble in the unlikely event that he was even charged with her death. They were in the African bush during wartime, with no law to speak of except martial law, which would always protect the military from any scandal. He could do whatever he wanted to her and get away with it. The thought made her want to scream at the injustice of it all, but instead, she began to weep like the pitiful creature she'd always sworn she would never be.

"Tears will not save you, but perhaps a good lashing and prayers to the almighty for your damned and immortal soul might," Roger said as he unbuckled his belt. "I had hoped to do this in the privacy of the bedroom, but since you have chosen not to take your punishment and salvation with feminine decorum, you leave me no choice but to do it here and now."

"There will be no such punishment," the Captain's voice rang out from the shadowy corners of the entrance hall.

"Interfering bastard!" Roger said. "What happens between a man and his wife is none of your concern, especially if the wife in question is a witch who needs to be put back on the path of righteousness."

"We all know that your plans for her have nothing to do with righteousness and everything to do with your iniquities as a man," the Captain said as he stepped out of the shadows, his hand on the pommel of his sabre.

Maretta allowed a sigh of relief to escape her lips, but the relief didn't last long. Only then did she notice Roger's hand on his service revolver. He hadn't removed it from his belt before the Captain interrupted him.

"That would be a bloody stupid thing to do, Lieutenant," the Captain said. "Considering your actions in the town today, the only reason you're not already in the stockade for violating the rules of engagement is Lord Roberts's longstanding friendship with your family, but even that won't save you from the firing squad if you pull that weapon."

"The witch has you under her spell. Can't you see that," Roger said.

"I suggest you let the lady go," the Captain said as he reached out to Maretta.

"She's no lady," Roger said as he grabbed her hair again. "She's a whore of Beelzebub and has been cavorting with demons. I've seen her with my very eyes. Can't you see I'm fighting for her soul?"

"I see a man who means to do his wife harm, and as a gentleman, I can't allow that," the Captain said as he took a step closer, one hand gripping his sabre and the other outstretched towards Maretta. "Unhand the lady and allow her to leave now."

Maretta reached towards him as Roger loosened his grip on her hair. The Captain pulled her towards him and out of Roger's reach. On unsteady legs, Maretta stumbled out into the bright sunshine.

"Mark my words, Captain," Roger said from inside the house, his words drifting to them on the breeze. "My wife is a witch, and by the time we reach Pretoria, everyone will know what she is, and they will hang her for it."

As the Captain led her away from the house and the aftermath of the carnage that had taken place there, Maretta couldn't help the chill that spread through her from Roger's prediction. Even the heat from the sun couldn't stop her shivering. The Captain's promises of protection couldn't stop her from wondering if Roger was right. Would she be hanged as a witch before they reached their destination?

The cottage on the inside was bigger than it appeared from the outside. While it had a roaring fire in its hearth and retained some of the charm Eithne remembered from her time, it also had all the modern conveniences she'd come to appreciate from Nick's apartment. There were even things she didn't recognise and vibrated at different frequencies from anything she'd encountered. She felt drawn to them. Her fingers tingled as she reached out to touch them.

"Look with your eyes, not your hands," Taranis said. "Those are not for you."

"Don't be such a selfish prick," Thandi said as she picked up a golden orb and tossed it from one hand to the other like a cat playing with a ball.

"That's not a toy," Taranis said as he plucked it out of the air mid-toss and put it back on a shelf with other objects that radiated strange energies. Some made Eithne want to run away, screaming never to return, while others enticed her senses and made her want to rub them all over her naked body.

"You never were any fun," Thandi said, distracting Eithne from a book that whispered to her.

"Wasn't it having *fun* that got you thrown out of Egypt?" Taranis said as he stepped in front of Thandi, preventing her from grabbing yet another object.

"I shouldn't be here," Maretta said, her energy pulsing in and out the closer she drifted to certain objects. "I'm not feeling right. There's something wrong."

"You need to be more specific," Taranis said. "Can you tell what is wrong or where this feeling emanates from? Only once you've narrowed it down can I help you."

"Well, this is familiar," Thandi said with a smirk. "Taranis rushing to Maretta's rescue without considering the consequences of his gallant deeds."

"Stop," Taranis said. "If you hadn't decided to show yourself and spit fire, none of that would have happened."

"I was hunted and shot at because of her," Thandi said, pointing a finger with a claw for a nail at Maretta.

"You're immortal, for fuck's sake," Maretta said. "Those bullets wouldn't have done anything to you. I died, so could we please keep some perspective about who had it worse the last time we were together? Okay?"

"Fine, but just for the record, those bullets really stung, and I have the scars to prove it."

"Seriously!" Maretta shouted as her form wavered between visible and invisible. "What part of I bloody died because of you two, don't you understand?"

"I don't understand any of it," Eithne said, her attention not fully on the bickering but being drawn towards the book and its whispers. Their voices drifted into the background and became a barely perceptible hum. The book's whispers grew louder and more insistent. The voices sounded familiar, as though she'd heard them in a dream. They beckoned to her, bidding her to remember them. They scratched at the corners of her memory, just out of reach.

A slight pressure began to build up behind her eyes. It was a sensation that Eithne had never felt before. The voices grew more and more insistent. The louder they got, the more her head ached, and her vision grew fuzzier. The room began to move around her, and her legs were no longer as steady as they had been just a few seconds before. She reached out towards the book, hoping that if she touched it, she would remember whatever it was they said she'd forgotten. If she could remember, perhaps the throbbing pain in her head would stop, and the room would stop moving.

Just as she was about to touch the book, a hand gripped her shoulder and pulled her away. The sudden disconnect from the whispering was jarring and painful as if the tendrils of a secret bond had been mercilessly severed, leaving her to ache for the embrace of an unknown truth forever out of reach.

"Don't listen to them," Taranis said as he looked down on her from what seemed to be a towering height. "Nothing they say is true. Their whispers will only end up trapping you again."

"Is that why they sound so familiar?" Eithne asked as she tried to shake the after-effects off.

"Not exactly the same as what Mael Muire used, but similar," Taranis said with a nod. "The runes Mael Muire used were older. The book is based on what she used."

"Why do you even have it?" Maretta asked, still struggling to keep her form.

"To study it, of course," Taranis said with a shrug.

"My Grandmother said a powerful book passed down through the generations had been lost in a fire when she was a girl and that the fire had been caused by a strange storm," Maretta said. "Given your predilection for storms and lightning, I'm guessing you had something to do with that fire and that the book was stolen and not lost in the flames."

Taranis smiled in response.

"Why are you so pissed off that he has the book? Should he have left the book in the hands of your ancestors?" Thandi asked. "So they could imprison any of us like they did Eithne? And who's to say that those of us who have disappeared over the centuries haven't been trapped by your family, and we don't know it? Although, I would have preferred that the book be destroyed. To be honest."

"Tried that," Taranis said. "It's fire and spell retardant."

"Seriously?" Thandi said. "Fucking witches!"

"Could we please go somewhere else?" Maretta begged. "Something here is making me feel very unwelcome."

"Please," Thandi said. "Like that's a new sensation."

"Do you believe this book could be used to imprison me again?"

"Not on its own, and it must be wielded by a living descendant of Mael Muire's and to my knowledge, that particular bloodline died out shortly after Maretta was killed.

She was the last female in that line, and her brothers only produced sons who didn't live long enough to have children of their own."

"Are you sure?" Eithne asked. "If there are any living descendants that can imprison me, I need to know."

"So you can kill them?" Maretta asked.

"Yes," Eithne said. "I need to eliminate any threat. I will not be imprisoned again."

"There's no need to worry. I kept an eye on that family for centuries, and that line has died out," Taranis said. "You need to focus on finding my sister."

"And what if you're wrong?" Eithne asked, not taking her eyes off the book.

"If a descendant did by some miracle slip past me, which I highly doubt, they would need that book, which is safe here," Taranis said. "Firstly, they would need to know where to find my temple, the location of which is only known to a few surviving family members. Then there are my wards and other sundry defences, both physical and magical. A living descendant of Mael Muire's can't get through them. As you can see from Maretta's reaction, who is here with my permission and already dead, the consequences of entering without my permission are deadly."

"That explains that, then," Maretta said.

"Satisfied?" Taranis asked Eithne, who finally managed to tear her eyes away from the book.

"Not really, but it will have to do for now," Eithne said. "Do you have any thoughts on where we should start looking for your sister?"

"I have a few leads," Taranis said. "The first is back at Thandi's shop and a certain Papa Ben."

"He's dead," Thandi said. "And considering what was done to him, I'm not sure he'll be much help."

"I know, which is why I need something from your shop," Taranis said as he picked up an item that resembled an ancient key, its tarnished surface hinting at forgotten ages. Closing the door to his cottage from the inside, he inserted the key into the keyhole and turned it. It was a simple action without any fanfare. There was no blinding light and no smoke.

Eithne found it a little disappointing. She'd always believed that the Gods and everything they did would be on a much grander scale. That they would be all-knowing and have the answers. But they turned out to be just as clueless as she was.

"Come on, Ladies," Taranis said as he opened the door. "This should be interesting."

Before any of them could ask a question, he was gone. Thandi shrugged and followed him. Maretta's flickering form drifted through the exit. Eithne sighed before she, too, walked through.

She felt as though she was mindlessly following someone she didn't know or trust and who, in turn, was blindly forging ahead without any real plan. In this journey of shadows and half-truths, she felt like a pawn on a board where the rules remained shrouded. The door closed, the transition seamless, and the world on the other side beckoned.

16

The journey across the Great Orange River Bridge was fraught with suspicion and fear. Some of the men who'd participated in Roger's slaughter of the Hope Town inhabitants had faced the consequences of following Roger's orders without question. They'd been mowed down by a firing squad moments before the rest of the army mobilised to cross the river and set off towards Kimberley to reinforce the soldiers under siege there. The remaining men who had taken part in Roger's atrocities buried their dead brethren while Roger rode out in disgrace but alive under the watchful gaze of Lord Roberts.

Maretta's face was still wet from the tears she'd shed for those men and herself as she left Hope Town. She'd watched them beg for their lives, much like the innocent women and children they'd killed had probably done. She cried for herself because Roger had proven he could get away with murder, and even though his men were punished for his orders, many of the other men seemed to feel that they'd been unjustly punished. They were at war, after all.

Before crossing the bridge, the Captain and his men, who seemed devout in their absolute loyalty to him, rechecked the bridge for any explosives. Since the bridge at Bethulie had been blown up by the Boers just a few days ago, the bridge was inspected more thoroughly before crossing. The news of the Bethulie bridge sabotage had reached Lord Roberts thanks to the modern marvel of the field telephone. She marvelled at the use of radio waves and the electric telegraph during their journey north. Even though it had been invented ten years ago, some people still considered it otherworldly. Maretta wasn't sure if she believed it was a scientific advancement or if Heinrich Hertz had figured out a way to harness the magic that was all around them.

"All clear," the Captain shouted, distracting her from her musings on magic and science and bringing her attention firmly to the unpleasant present and her predicament.

As the army trudged wearily across the bridge, a suffocating tension clung to the air like a vice grip. The planks groaned beneath the weight of both marching boots and wagons. Hushed whispers drifted through the ranks. They carried a weight far heavier than artillery.

These were no longer mere murmurs of camaraderie but urgent, furtive exchanges that danced on the fringes of audibility. A storm of emotions simmered below the surface – a volatile concoction of pent-up anger, gnawing fear, and smouldering resentment. Some of her wanted to believe that it was Eithne's doing, but she couldn't help but wonder if something else was at play. The atmosphere trembled with the explosive energy of potent emotions that threatened to ignite like a tinderbox at the slightest provocation.

She got a glimpse of Roger's face as she crossed into the Boer Republic. She'd thought he would have looked contrite so soon after witnessing his men being executed, but instead, he wore a smug look of superiority on his face, as though he'd won some victory instead of narrowly avoiding his own execution.

The word Witch danced on the air towards her. Then she understood why he looked so smug. He hadn't wasted any time putting his plans for her future, or lack thereof, into action. His defence for his actions was her downfall, and his siege on her life had begun. Another word drifted on the air – whore. His attack on the Captain was also clear to see for anyone paying attention. The Captain at least had his men to protect his honour, but if he kept coming to her rescue, it would only fuel the flames. Like Hawthorne's Hester Prynne, she too would be branded with a scarlet letter if she was lucky, but she doubted Roger would be placated with a simple letter being embroidered on her clothes.

Maretta watched in trepidation as the Captain rode towards her. Hostile eyes moved with him along the flank of the marching army.

"You need to stay away from me," Maretta said as he pulled his horse up alongside her wagon.

"I only wanted to enquire about your well-being, Madam," the Captain said with an overly formal tone and loud enough for curious ears to hear.

"As you can see, I'm perfectly fine and have no need of your assistance," Maretta said, matching his tone and volume.

"I take it you've heard the not-so-subtle whispers going around," he said, lowering his voice.

"I have," Maretta said, lowering her voice and eyes. She didn't want him to see the tears threatening her resolve to be strong.

"I'm sorry," he said. "I didn't think he would act this quickly or that so many would believe him after his actions at Hope Town."

"Then you're more naïve than I thought you were," Maretta said as a sad smile touched her lips. "This wasn't something he did overnight. My husband has been sowing those seeds for some time now. The lives of the men lost at sea during the storm and those men whose executions you sanctioned this morning have become the nutrients that finally allowed his seeds to take root and begin to grow. Hopefully, a Boer bullet will find its mark, and I'll be saved."

"Careful," he said. "If anything did befall him, with the current sentiments, you would most certainly be blamed."

"I'm not a witch," Maretta said. "I don't really know what I am."

"Mores the pity," the Captain said. "If you were a witch and as powerful as your ancestor, you'd be able to conjure your way out of this mess."

"What the devil do you know about my family?" Maretta said as the Captain spurred his horse into motion and galloped away, leaving Maretta alone with her fears.

She could feel the watchful eyes of the soldiers on her. How many whispered words of their conversation had been carried away by the wind to those hungry ears, and how long would it take for those words to travel to Roger, who was no doubt eager for any ammunition he could use against her and the Captain?

The oxen trudged before her as she tried to ignore those hostile glances. She stared at their rumps as they swayed with each step they took. She realised she still didn't know his name, who he was or how he fit into her family's drama. Could she trust a man whose name she didn't know? The thought that her life was in his hands filled her with even more trepidation. Then there was Alistair, and the knowledge that Roger knew of him scared her more than she wanted to admit. What would Roger do to him should he find Alistair before she did?

Maretta's gaze remained steady on the horizon, where strange storm clouds began to build up, echoing the events unfolding around her. Her heartbeat harmonised with the march as the army strode towards the storm, each beat a reminder of her chosen path.

Roger's presence lingered like a spectre, poisoning every thought and step of those around her. His weapons were cruel words—accusations of witchery and whoredom—a dark reflection of the power he wielded.

Within the ceaseless rhythm of rain, Maretta's resolve found its anchor. The Captain's intentions remained veiled; Alistair's fate was a mystery, but her own path was clear. Protecting the world from Eithne was her solemn duty and the only thing that mattered. No matter what Roger tried to do to her, Eithne had to stay in her coffin. If she were to rise, the consequences would be dire for the world and every living creature.

Thunder mingled with the cadence of her heart, a reminder that she was part of something larger. Her family and the legacy bestowed upon her might not be what she would have chosen for herself, but it was her burden to carry.

And so, as the storm raged on, Maretta pressed ahead. The rain washed away doubts, leaving in their wake a determination that burned brighter with each passing moment. The road ahead promised challenges and revelations, but Maretta was determined to face them.

Eithne exited the door to find Taranis rummaging through the shelves of Thandi's shop. Maretta's diaphanous form no longer flickered in and out of existence. Eithne wasn't entirely sure how she felt that Maretta's spirit was once again at full strength, especially since she now knew of a book that could once again imprison her. Despite Taranis' assurances that there wasn't a living member of Mael Muire's bloodline, Eithne couldn't shake the feeling that leaving the book unguarded would one day return to bite her in the arse.

"Could you be more careful," Thandi yelled as a ceramic jar fell to the floor and shattered, distracting Eithne's thoughts from the book. "That shit's expensive."

"Sorry," Taranis said but continued to ransack her shop.

"Maybe if you tell me what you're looking for, I could help, and you wouldn't need to fuck up my shop to find it," Thandi said as she tried to put things back where she wanted them.

"I can't," Taranis said as a glass bottle filled with an unknown clear, viscous liquid toppled over, and its contents dripped onto the floor at Thandi's tapping bare foot.

"It's a good thing I'm not human because if I were, I wouldn't have a foot anymore," Thandi said as she glared at

Taranis, who ignored her. "Just tell me what you're looking for so this can stop."

"I can't," Taranis said again.

"What do you mean 'You can't'?" Eithne asked, interrupting Thandi, who was about to ask the same thing.

"I don't know what it is," Taranis said as he moved to another shelf. "I know it's here, and I'll know it when I touch it."

"Whatever happened to looking with your eyes?" Maretta asked.

"I have to touch it to know if it resonates with Cailleach," Taranis said as he picked up a shrunken head whose small beady eyes popped open, and its mouth formed a silent scream as he threw it over his shoulder.

"Did you have to throw him that hard," Thandi said. "He has feelings, too, you know."

"Yes, very violent ones," Taranis said as he unconsciously wiped his hands on his kilt. "I can sense her presence here. She left an imprint behind on something, and I think she did so that I could find her someday."

"I thought you said it had to do with Papa Ben," Thandi said.

"It does, and it doesn't," Taranis said.

"What the fuck is that supposed to mean," Thandi said.

"I know Papa Ben had something in his possession at some point that could have been from Cailleach that he stole from another witch."

"In other words, you don't actually have any clue as to what you're looking for," Maretta said. "How typical of you to rush in without any plan and expect everything to fall into place."

"This is not the time to bring up mistakes that anyone could have made," Taranis said as yet another object flew across the shop.

"But you're not just anyone, now are you," Maretta said. "You're the bloody God of Thunder who thought masquerading around as a Captain in the British army was a great idea."

Their usual bickering faded into a hum once more as Eithne was distracted by the salty scent of the ocean and the sound of crashing waves. A warm, glowing feeling pulled her to the back of Thandi's shop. It was a feeling of hope, new beginnings, and adventure. It beckoned to her from a smooth stone with runes carved into its surface that had been rolled and sanded by millennia of ocean tides.

"Are you sure she left it for you to find," Maretta asked as she glanced towards Eithne, who had wandered away from them and was holding the ancient stone.

"I always thought it would be for me, but now that you mention it, she could have left breadcrumbs for Eithne to follow should she one day rise," Taranis said as he stroked his beard.

"What is this?" Eithne asked. "It feels so familiar, but I've never seen anything like it."

"It's a rune stone," Thandi said as she made her way to Eithne and reached to touch the ancient stone. "But I've never seen it before. I didn't even know it was here."

"What does it say?" Maretta asked.

"The lines are hard to read," Taranis said as he looked over Eithne's shoulder.

"They're perfectly clear to me," Eithne said as she read the words that quickened her heartbeat.

"Where sun's embrace kisses sands,
In shadows cast, a pathway's trace.
Seek astral guide when stars align,
To waters where two worlds entwine.
From lion's realm to eagle's view,
Follow whispers. They'll guide you through.
Seven steps through moonlit haze,
To veil between where mortals gaze.
Underneath the Great Serpent's eye,
Through ancient dunes where secrets lie,
Beyond horizons, spirits roam,
Where waves embrace the mystic's home.
Unveil the mirror of the night,
When Southern Cross points pure and bright.
Let heart and spirit intertwine,
To Tír na nÓg, elusive, divine."

"What does that even mean?" Maretta asked no one in particular.

"It means we're going to Tír na nÓg, the land of the young, the realm of eternal youth and beauty," Taranis said.

"Great," Thandi said. "I guess we're going home. The one place we swore we'd never go back to."

"Looks like," Taranis said.

"Fuck," Thandi said.

17

The strange thunderstorm had long since passed, leaving an oppressive heat in its place. The open veld spotted with camel thorn trees stretched out before her. Hope Town and the Orange River bridge lay a few days in her past, but the events still followed Maretta with a dogged determination. She couldn't shake the feeling that she was being watched, even though the soldiers' hushed whispers and curious stares had dwindled somewhat as their focus shifted northward. The march toward Magersfontein consumed their attention as they advanced under the orders of Lord Roberts. The target was the town, tantalisingly close to Kimberley—a prize to be seized, a stronghold to be claimed. It would still take many days to reach, though. Not even Lord Roberts could command the army to march faster than they already were.

The Captain had also thankfully respected her wishes to stay away from her and prevented any more rumours about them that could add fuel to Roger's slander, but the feeling that something was amiss still tingled at the back of her neck. She might not be a powerful witch like the other women in her family, but she could still sense things. The Orange River crossing and the strange storm that had enveloped them shortly after whispered of supernatural powers at play.

As a slight breeze played with the long grass, a shimmer appeared on the horizon, almost like a mirage in the desert, but that didn't belong in the lush veld that spread out around her. A few of the soldiers marching near her also seemed to notice the strange shimmer but seemed to put it down to too much sun, rubbing their eyes and looking away. A few crossed themselves and spat. The superstitious gesture was a reminder of the precariousness of her particular situation. If anything peculiar happened, no matter how insignificant, it would be seen as evidence of witchcraft and play into Roger's hands.

The sound of distant flowing water drifted towards her. They hadn't seen another river since crossing the bridge and would need to find more water soon if they didn't want the animals to start dropping like flies. A soldier marching nearby licked his lips and started looking around as though he, too, had heard the water.

"There is water close," a whispered voice said. "Gariep will take you to it."

"Who said that?" Maretta whispered back.

"I didn't say anything, Your Ladyship," a young foot soldier marching next to her wagon said with a confused look.

"Gariep said it," the voice whispered again. Dark, curious eyes appeared in the shimmering mirage, which had drifted closer to her and now hovered beside her wagon.

"Wonderful!" Maretta said. "Now everyone will truly think I've lost my senses."

"Pardon my Lady," the young soldier said. "Is something amiss?"

"Thank you for your concern. It was a passing moment of confusion, probably due to the heat. I appreciate your kindness," Maretta said, trying to downplay the moment and keep some measure of composure. The last thing she needed was for him to run off to tell anyone she'd been speaking to strange entities floating next to her.

"It's not far," the voice whispered again. "If you follow, Gariep will lead you to it."

"I'm not following you anywhere," Maretta whispered back, hoping the soldier wouldn't hear her.

"Gariep does not wish you harm, Guardian," the entity whispered. "Gariep only seeks to help you."

"Why do you call me Guardian?" Maretta said.

"Are you not the Guardian of She Who Sleeps?"

"Guardian," Maretta said. "I suppose that is one way of looking at it."

"If you will not follow Gariep," the entity said. "Gariep can bring a soft rain for you to drink. Would that make you happy, Guardian?"

"That is a very kind offer," Maretta said. "But could you please go away before anyone else sees or hears you?"

"Why would you want Gariep to go away?" the entity asked with a hurt tone. "Gariep only wishes to serve She Who Sleeps and her Guardian."

"Gariep," Maretta said. "Is that your name?"

"Yes, Guardian of She Who Sleeps," Gariep said. "Gariep, like you, is a Guardian. Gariep is the Guardian of the Great River. Gariep is here to help you on your journey."

"That is very kind of you, Gariep," Maretta whispered, looking around to ensure the soldier wasn't listening. She was thirsty and knew the soldiers were too. "A gentle rain to fill our water canteens and water the animals would be nice."

"Gariep is mighty," Gariep said as clouds began to gather overhead and a slight drizzle began to fall. "Gariep sends you nice rain."

The oxen began to moo happily as the light rain lowered the temperature and stopped the flies from buzzing around their eyes and mouths. The soldiers also began to enjoy the break from the heat. Some opened their mouths to drink the nourishing liquid and filled their tin canteens that were close to empty. The two pints they carried never did last long and would need to be filled again soon.

Maretta's parasol, which had been used to fend off the blazing sun, was now helping to keep the rain from drenching her clothes. It was one of the items that Roger had thought her ridiculous for bringing but had proven to be the most useful.

She smiled at the enjoyment the rain brought to most of the soldiers marching north; the young foot soldier walking next to her wagon, on the other hand, looked at her with suspicion. Amidst the raindrops, an unspoken threat hung heavy. Maretta's smile faltered, and her heart began to beat a nervous staccato. She couldn't help but wonder how much he had heard of her request to Gariep and if it could be construed as witchcraft. If he told Roger about what he'd heard, just the slightest hint of the otherworldly would be enough to seal her fate.

The stone was warm in Eithne's hands, and its message glowed. Tír na nÓg was only ever whispered about when she was a child. It was feared that travelling to the otherworld would bring a curse down through the ages of anyone who dared trespass in the land beyond the veil. Even though she'd joined the ranks of immortals, the thought of crossing into their domain filled her with the same awe she had felt sitting at her father's feet as he told the stories of the Sidhe. She could still see his scraggly red beard with strands of grey in the firelight of his Crannóg as his deep voice mingled with the sounds of the loch. The memory of her long-dead father brought a smile to her lips, but with the smile also came a bitter sadness. She would never see him again or hear him tell his tales.

"How do we get there?" Maretta asked. Her voice brought Eithne out of memories and reminded her that there were answers to be sought.

"My temple in the desert," Thandi said. "There's a portal to the Grove there."

"Why don't I know about this portal?" Taranis said.

"Don't you have your own portal?" Thandi said.

"You know I closed it centuries ago," Taranis said. "Remember that whole pact we made about never going back there?"

"So I kept mine open just in case," Thandi said. "And look, we need it now. So, instead of getting all pissy about it, how about you say thank you for keeping a back door open and not being an idiot? Is that too much to ask?"

"You know what, I'm not going to get into it with you," Taranis said. "Can we just get going so we can get this over and done with?"

"Fine," Thandi said as she opened the door at the back of her store again, only instead of opening onto a green field dotted with grazing sheep, they were hit with a blast of heat and sand.

"I fucking hate this place," Thandi said as they exited the door in front of a stone temple that looked like it had been forgotten by the ages. Desert sand blew all around them, whipping their legs and arms.

"Isn't it *your* temple?" Maretta asked. "So, don't you get to decide what it's like?"

"It used to be great," Thandi said. "There was this beautiful oasis, and women came from all over Egypt to ask me for help and protection, but then my fucking brothers decided that everything had to be moved to Karnak, and all I got was a hidden away shrine there. I kept this place just for me and as a reminder of what bastards my brothers are. Horus got to keep his fucking temple, but I wasn't allowed to. Talk about double standards." She shook her head. "Men."

"I didn't realise you were Egyptian," Maretta said.

"There's a lot you don't know," Thandi said with a flick of her braids.

"Clearly," Maretta said. "So, which Egyptian deity are you supposed to be?"

"What do you mean 'supposed to be'?" Thandi asked with a hint of indignation. "I would have thought the whole transforming into a fire-breathing lioness would have made it pretty obvious."

"She's Sekhmet," Taranis said as he strode towards the temple's entrance, leaving them in the shadow of Thandi's shop door that was still open.

"Just don't fucking call me that, okay," Thandi said. "I left that name and everything that went with it when I left this place behind me."

"And yet you still turn into a big cat and breathe fire," Maretta said as she drifted towards where Taranis had gone.

"That's not something I can just turn off," Thandi said. "It's part of who I am. You understand that, right?" She said to Eithne, who shrugged and followed the others, leaving Thandi to close the door.

After the heat and billowing sand, the temple was surprisingly cold and quiet. Their footsteps echoed in the ancient halls. Faded murals told stories of Sekhmet's past. They called her by different names, like The Terrible One and Beloved of Ptah.

"Who is this Ptah they refer to here?" Eithne asked as she paused in front of a mural depicting Sekhmet as a wife and mother wearing a crown with a disk and a coiled cobra.

"My fucking ex," Thandi said. "Can we just move on? I don't want to discuss it, okay?"

"But what about your child?" Maretta asked as she drifted to where Eithne stood to examine the mural.

"You're probably about to find out," Thandi said as she walked past them towards a glowing, round pool of water at the heart of the temple. "The last I saw them, they were having an orgy with a couple of wood Nymphs in the Grove."

"You don't have to come with us," Taranis said.

"It's time I faced them," Thandi said with a sigh, stepped into the pool and vanished.

"I guess we're going for a swim," Taranis said, jumping in.

Maretta and Eithne stood together on the threshold of the portal, unsure of what awaited them on the other side.

"Must you really follow me everywhere?" Eithne asked with a hint of annoyance.

"Yes, unfortunately," Maretta said. "That is my curse to bear. I'm bound to you for all eternity. I'm stuck wherever you go."

"I see," Eithne said, staring into the pool. "I'd hoped you were lying about that."

"Unfortunately not, and trust me, I hate being here with you as much as you do," Maretta said with a quivering voice. "There are other people I want to spend my afterlife with."

"Perhaps if we find Cailleach, she'll be able to undo whatever was done to bind us together."

"Maybe, but I doubt it."

"I have to believe that she had a reason for creating me," Eithne said. "I have to believe that there is a reason I was locked in a box and that I've been freed in this strange world where nothing makes sense because if there's no reason for it, this rage I'm feeling will overwhelm me completely, and I don't know what will become of me if that happens."

"I won't let that happen," Maretta said, reaching an ephemeral hand out in a gesture of support.

"So we're in this together whether we like it or not," Eithne said as she wiped a tear off her cheek.

Maretta nodded.

"Then we should probably get going," Eithne said as she jumped into the portal with no thought of what might be on the other side except the hope of answers and her need to confront the Goddess who had started all of it.

18

Magersfontein was in sight, and the battle plans had been drawn. The water spirit, who called itself Gariep, had been true to his word and led them to water whenever needed, whispering directions in her ear, which she could use without attracting too much notice. The young foot soldier gave her the occasional strange look but hadn't sounded the alarm that she was talking to otherworldly familiars or screamed witchcraft, which gave Maretta hope that perhaps he hadn't heard her hushed conversations.

As the sun began to set, soldiers prepared themselves for the attack. Rifles and bayonets were cleaned. Ammunition was checked, and prayers were said. Letters to loved ones were written in case the worst should happen and given to friends with a promise that the letters would find their way home.

Roger had spent his time with the officers receiving orders and the terms of engagement, while Maretta spent her time at the field hospital making sure there were clean bandages, that surgical equipment was sterilised and that they would be ready for any wounded soldiers. The Captain had spent his time with Lord Roberts adjusting their strategies and stayed well away from her. Now, all they had to do was wait for the cover of darkness. The waiting was always the hardest.

Gariep grumbled about the army as he followed her around the camp. As time wore on, he grew more and more agitated. He felt that some of the men amongst them had evil intentions. She tried not to react to his comments as he lamented the state of Eithne and how he wished she could wake up.

"These men you travel with are a plague of locusts on this land," Gariep said as the moon rose and the men made their final preparations. "They have no respect and have befouled Gariep's rivers, which Gariep led them to. Gariep should not have helped them. Now, they will spill more blood, poisoning the great mother that feeds us all. Gariep can sense the blood fever amongst them. Gariep cannot let this happen."

"Please," Maretta said. "Don't do anything to interfere. They need this victory."

"Why do you serve these men, Guardian?" Gariep asked. "Gariep has seen how they look upon you and She Who Sleeps with fear."

"I travel with them because I must," Maretta said. "I'm looking for someone, and I think if I can get to Pretoria, I will find him."

"You are on the wrong path, Guardian," Gariep said with sadness. "Gariep is sad because Gariep was wrong about you."

"Why do you say that?"

"You are not her Guardian," Gariep said as the sadness turned to anger. "The voices told Gariep who you are. You are the one who holds her captive, and you and all those who mean her harm must be stopped. Gariep knows what he must do."

"Gariep, please let me explain," Maretta said a little louder than she had wanted as the water spirit disappeared, swallowed by the darkening dusk. The same soldier who seemed to dog her every step of late was again in earshot and frowned as he was called into formation along with the rest of his platoon.

The night was eerily quiet. The sounds of crickets and laughing hyenas that usually added their voices to the African bush's symphony that Maretta had grown accustomed to were suddenly silent. It was as though the conductor had waved his baton to hush them all. A mist began to form as the men joined ranks, ready to attack. The terrain was tricky under normal circumstances, but the rocky ground and scrubby vegetation covered by the ever-thickening mist would make it harder for the soldiers to see the enemy, let alone not break a leg before firing a shot.

The undercurrent of nervous tension among the soldiers was palpable. Maretta's heart quickened as the whispered order to advance filtered through the sea of men that moved as one. It didn't take long for the battlefield to erupt into a vortex of confusion and despair as the carefully laid plans unravelled and the grim toll of war began to claim its merciless dues. The deafening percussion of gunshots and the piercing wails of the wounded and dying saturated the stifling air, weaving a tapestry of unrelenting chaos and despair.

Wounded soldiers carrying their dead and dying friends to the field hospital were followed by news of the Boer ambush filtering through the encampment. The enemy had dug trenches that had been covered by the terrain and the thick mist. They'd been lying in wait to pick them off. Seven hundred men lay dying on the battlefield. As the dying men's screams echoed through the British army, punctured by the victory celebrations of the Boer commandoes, questions began to be asked. How had the Boers known they were coming? How could a bunch of farmers beat the strongest army in the world? Where had the strange mist come from?

The survivors who weren't in the hospital tent fighting for their lives huddled around their cooking fires and began to whisper amongst themselves. Someone had to be to blame for their friends who had died. They claimed they could all feel the unseen hostility permeating the air they breathed. They soon began to assemble in bigger groups as the whispers grew louder.

Maretta watched the gathering maelstrom from the entrance of the surgical station tent. The screams of the young soldier whose leg was being amputated and the surgeon's calls for help were muted as Roger waded through the soldiers, gathering them in his wake.

"She did this," Roger's voice cut through their angry shouts for answers and someone to blame like a whip cracking the air. He stood taller than Maretta had ever seen him before. It was as though the moment he'd been waiting for gave him that extra gravitas he'd always lacked. He took on a false air of righteous indignation, and with fiery determination in his eyes, he ignited a frenzy among the men.

She felt their rough hands grab her and drag her out of the tent. The surgeon was torn between saving the screaming soldier on his operating table and trying to save Maretta from the raging mob of soldiers. Ultimately, the Doctor chose to save the life he could. Maretta couldn't blame him for the choice he made. She knew the moment she saw the young foot soldier by Roger's side, her fate was sealed.

"I heard her talking to a spirit the whole way here," the young soldier said. "It was her witch's familiar who caused that unnatural mist."

"Listen to him," Roger said. "This young man speaks the truth. He's seen her witchery with his own eyes and heard her casting spells, and he's not alone. I've seen her communing with unnatural spirits. She spoke to a fire-breathing lion and set it upon me. She carries that cursed Kist with her wherever she goes. It brings chaos and doom to all of us. Remember that cursed storm that followed us to these shores and the men who died at sea. She sacrificed them to her pagan gods."

His fervent words painted a portrait of betrayal and dark sorcery. "The mist that ensured our defeat was no mere weather phenomenon," he proclaimed, "but the sinister work of this witch who conspired against our mighty army. Her sorcery knows no bounds and must be stopped."

Maretta's heart raced as the soldiers all nodded in agreement with everything he said.

"Stop this insanity," the Captain's voice rang out.

"Seize him," Roger shouted. "He is her lover and is under her spell."

"Don't listen to this madness," the Captain said. "You men know me. I'm telling you the Lieutenant has his own aims in mind here, and they have nothing to do with our defeat this night. He is a disgruntled and abusive husband whose wife doesn't want to be beaten any more. There is nothing sinister about this woman. She's a nurse who has helped and healed many of you after a battle. On the other hand, he is responsible for the massacre at Hope Town and the execution of his men. He is a coward and a liar. I implore you don't help him commit this atrocity against an innocent woman."

"You can't save your lover," Roger said as he shoved the Captain. "She's a witch, and you know it. She's in league with the Devil, a whore of Beelzebub. We can all see her for what she is."

"Stop this," a commanding voice came out of the dark. "I will not have my army torn apart."

"My Lord," Roger said with a bow as Lord Roberts strode out of the night.

"If your wife is indeed what you claim, she will be tried in accordance with our laws. We will not have a lynching; is that understood?"

"Yes, my Lord," Robert said with a bow of his head.

"Enough blood has been spilt here," Lord Roberts said as he eyed Maretta with sympathy. "Let her go."

"With respect, my Lord," Roger said. "She can't be left to her own devices. What if she runs off and joins the enemy? What if, because of your lack of belief in her powers, she casts more spells and more innocent lives are lost? The men would blame you, my Lord."

"I see," Lord Roberts said. "What would you have me do?"

"For the sake of the men, put her in irons," Roger said. "They say that iron affects her kind."

"Very well," Lord Roberts said.

"You can't be serious," the Captain said. "This is ridiculous."

"Captain," Lord Roberts said in hushed tones as he pulled the Captain away from the rest of the crowd. Maretta had to strain her ears to hear what was said over the angry declarations from the mob. "I suggest you stay clear of this matter. Your interest in this woman has reached even my ears. You do her no favours by attempting to be her champion. If she is innocent, and I'm sure these charges are as ridiculous as you say, she will be found so in a court of law. But for the sake of morale, we must do this."

"My Lord," the Captain said. "May I have a moment alone with her."

"That would be ill-advised," Lord Roberts said. "You and I both know that her husband would take umbrage with that and add fuel to the fire. Stay away from her."

"Please, my Lord," the Captain begged. "Just a few moments."

"Are you really that besotted with her that you would risk your life and career for a short exchange of words?"

"I can assure you, my Lord, that there is nothing untoward between myself and the Lady. I wish to reassure the poor woman who is most assuredly afraid and needs reassurance that all is not lost."

"I cannot give you a moment alone; that would be too noticeable, but I can distract the Lieutenant and the men for a few moments while you have your little tête-à-tête."

"Thank you, my Lord," the Captain said with a grateful sigh.

Two soldiers clapped irons around her wrists and ankles connected by a thick chain.

"Gather round, gentlemen," Lord Roberts said with a voice accustomed to commanding thousands of men's attention. "We must put these sordid details and this tragic loss behind us as we set our sights on the future and Kimberley. This has no doubt been a great loss, but it is one that we shall overcome."

His voice faded into the background as Maretta focused on the Captain and the feeling of the iron cuffs against her skin. It was a strange sensation. She'd never put much stock in what she'd always thought of as an old wives tale that her mother and all her ancestors had perpetuated. Even though they'd used iron to put Eithne down all those generations ago, she'd always thought Eithne didn't rise because of the runes carved into the wood of her coffin. But as she began to feel weaker, she realised the truth behind it. It was also a surprise that the iron affected her at all since she'd always thought she was an ordinary mortal, unlike the rest of her family. If she shared their weaknesses, did she also share their strengths?

"I'm so sorry," the Captain said. "Are you alright?"

"This isn't my usual sort of jewellery," Maretta said, wriggling her wrists and trying to make light of the situation as she felt weaker with every passing second.

"The iron is affecting you, isn't it?" the Captain asked.

Maretta managed to nod.

"I can't let him see me fall," Maretta said as she focused on staying on her feet. "I need you to look after the Kist for me. It can't fall into the wrong hands."

"What makes you so sure I'm not the wrong hands?" the Captain asked.

"If you were, she would already be free, and I would be dead."

"I'll take care of her," the Captain promised. "Is there anything else I can do for you?"

"You could tell me who you are," Maretta said with a weak smile.

"Stay alive, and I'll tell you," the Captain said with a wink and was swallowed up by the night and the glow from the campfires.

Maretta stared at the unforgiving iron cuffs binding her wrists and waited to be dragged to whatever fresh hell Roger had planned for her. She knew that what waited for her at the end of their journey had nothing to do with some perverted sense of justice or her being a witch; it was a manifestation of Roger's twisted desire to inflict suffering on her, his unyielding thirst to make her atone for her imagined sins. As the dawn began to break and injured soldiers cried out in pain, Maretta steeled herself for the harrowing trials ahead, a prisoner to Roger's insidious vendetta.

Birds chatted in exotic trees while a gentle breeze played with perfect blades of grass. They stood around the portal they'd come through, dripping wet, in the middle of an orchard. Branches hung heavy with every imaginable type of fruit anyone could possibly want to eat. Eithne reached out to pluck a ripe pear from one of the branches.

"I wouldn't do that if I were you," Thandi said.

"Why?" Eithne asked.

"You want to leave here and find answers and things, don't you?" Thandi asked.

Eithne nodded.

"If you eat the fruit, you'll never want to leave. It's part of the magic of the place."

"Oh," Eithne said as she retracted her hand. "Pity, they all look delicious."

"They are," Taranis said as he licked his lips with longing.

Sounds of laughter tickled the air as running footsteps came towards them.

"Here we go," Thandi said with a sigh. "The happiness brigade is coming."

The giggling couple burst into the clearing.

"Welcome," the young wood Nymph with a crown of flowers woven into her hair said with a smile.

"We love newcomers," said the Satyr with a wink. A ring of flowers dangled from one of his horns. He gave Eithne and Maretta a lecherous once over, ignoring Taranis and Thandi.

"Oh, for fuck's sake," Thandi said.

"Relax, Kitty Cat and retract those claws," the Satyr said.

"Don't call me Kitty Cat, you lascivious goatling," Thandi said with clenched fists.

"We've missed you," the wood Nymph said.

"I can't say the same," Thandi said with a growl.

"Ptah and Tem will be happy to see you," the wood Nymph said with a sly smile.

"One more word and I will rip your throat out," Thandi said with a step towards the Nymph who hid behind the Satyr.

"You need to get laid," the Satyr said.

"Maybe you should take us to where Ptah and Tem are lounging about," Taranis said. "Or if you know where Cailleach is, just take us to her instead."

"She's not here," the Nymph said, peeking out from behind the Satyr.

"She has to be," Eithne said.

"We haven't seen her in years," the Satyr said.

"So, she was here?" Taranis asked.

"I vaguely remember seeing her at a party a few years ago," the Nymph said.

"Oh yes," the Satyr said. "She threw a hissy fit and stormed off quite literally. We got drenched that night."

"Didn't she hit Brigid with a lightning bolt during her poetry recital?" the Nymph asked the Satyr.

"That was funny," the Satyr started laughing at the memory. "Brigid's poem was horrendous."

"Really?" the Nymph asked. "I thought it was quite sweet. Could have been a bit shorter, but it was cute."

"A bit shorter?" the Satyr asked. "It was over an hour long. When that bolt hit Brigid, I wanted to kiss Cailleach full on her thin, angry lips."

"She would have killed you for just having that thought," Taranis said.

"Now, that's something I would have paid to see," Thandi said.

"What happened after she stormed off?" Eithne asked. "Did you see where she went or if she spoke to anyone?"

The Satyr and the Nymph both shrugged. Eithne sighed.

"Just take us to whoever might have some sort of idea where Cailleach might have gone," Eithne said as she tried to control her urge to throw a fireball at them.

"Most of them are gathered at Bacchus's place. The Muses are putting on a play," the Nymph said. "It should be fun."

"There'll be wine," the Satyr said as he turned and pulled the Nymph along with him.

"Great," Thandi said as she followed the others. "I'm going to need a lot of wine to deal with Bacchus and those fucking Muses."

"You didn't need to come," Maretta said. "You could have stayed behind and saved us all from having to listen to you bitch about how much you hate paradise and all the immortal beings who choose to be happy here."

"You have no idea why I hate this place or what happened to me here, so how about you shove your judgement up your prissy little dead arse and shut the fuck up," Thandi said as she strode ahead of the rest of them. "I'll be at the bar downing shots," she shouted over her shoulder.

"At least you guys can drink," Maretta said softly with a sigh as she floated between Eithne and Taranis.

"I'm sorry," Taranis said. "I only ever tried to help you. I hope you know that."

"I know," Maretta said. "What happened wasn't your fault. The day I married Roger was the day my death began. He was always going to kill me. My family's ambition always blinded them to the inevitable end of our bloodline, and to be honest, considering everything they did with their power, I can't say it's a bad thing. All their plotting and scheming led to absolutely nothing except the end of Mael Muire's dynasty."

"I wish I could have been there to see her die," Eithne said. "How did she die, by the way?"

"I don't know," Maretta said. "It was two thousand years ago. The only reason she's even remembered now is because each generation had to look after your body. No one kept records of her life after she cursed you and gave birth to Giric's daughter. The little we do know is nothing more than family legend, and most of that has been forgotten and warped through the ages."

"A daughter," Eithne said with a smile. "That would have made Giric very unhappy. He only ever wanted sons."

"Do you know how she died," Maretta asked Taranis.

"Now that you mention it, I don't," Taranis said with a frown. "I'd assumed it was of old age, which in those days would probably have been around forty or that she died of some plague or in a battle with another tribe or the Romans. There are so many ways she could have died."

"But she is dead," Eithne said. "You're sure of this, right?"

"Of course, she's dead," Maretta said. "She didn't turn herself into some immortal witch, did she?"

"Of course she's dead," Taranis said. "If she were still alive, we would know about it. Someone powerful enough to become immortal would leave a huge footprint through time."

"Neither of you sounds very sure," Eithne said. "Now we need to find Cailleach even more. Perhaps she will know what happened to Mael Muire and where her body is so I can spit on what's left of her bones and put her behind me once and for all."

As they walked towards the temple of Bacchus, the sounds of drunken laughter punched the ambrosial air. A gnawing uncertainty clung to Eithne like a shadow. Mael Muire, being dead and buried, her bones turned to nothing but ash, had been a source of comfort for her. But now, the uncertainty of her demise and the possibility that perhaps she would still get to have her revenge on the woman who had caused her so much pain gave Eithne some new and unexpected hope. She smiled as she pushed open the ancient doors to the temple. Cailleach still needed to be found, and questions needed to be answered, but first, she would get incredibly drunk.

19

After months of confinement, locked in a small cage with thick iron bars, Maretta could barely stand. They'd at least removed the cuffs from her wrists and ankles. Pins and needles in her extremities reminded her that she was at least still alive. The young soldier who'd told them of her conversations with Gariep had been put in charge of her as he'd proven unsusceptible to her witchery. They bounced over the uneven terrain as they headed to a farm on the outskirts of Pretoria. She couldn't help but wonder if the boy was purposefully going over every rock he could find. Even though Roger hadn't been able to beat her while she was imprisoned, the iron bars had left their mark much the same way his belt would have.

She hadn't seen Gariep since the loss at Magersfontein. Although she hadn't been seen to have any more conversations with what the men called her familiar, the damage had been done. The men had taken their recent victories over the Boer soldiers at Paardeberg and Poplar Grove as proof that she had been in league with the Devil. The Captain hadn't been allowed near her as they feared he would free her, so she only hoped that the Captain had been true to his words and had taken charge of Eithne's body and that she hadn't been set free.

After Magersfontein, Lord Roberts had sent Major-General French and his cavalry off on a daring expedition to Kimberley with the instruction that he must relieve the town even if it cost him half his forces. Maretta had been disappointed that Roger had not gone with Major-General French but had stayed with the main force, taking Bloemfontein. If he'd accompanied the Major-General, he might not have survived, and she might have been spared the discomfort she'd had to endure.

Johannesburg and all its gold were now in British hands. Only the Boer Capital of Pretoria needed to be taken. Lord Roberts would ride through the streets in a parade while the Boer leadership had scattered. They hadn't surrendered as he'd hoped and would probably attack again and disrupt supply lines. His parade through the city was a hollow victory. It was also something that Maretta wouldn't see. Roger had made his own plans while Lord Roberts was distracted.

The farm's owners had been carted off to a concentration camp, and the house had been turned into a garrison for Roger's surviving squad members and the foot soldier who had joined Roger. He refused to give her his name because he was afraid that it was knowledge she could use to bewitch him and turn him into her slave. The fact that she'd heard the other men call him John was neither here nor there. The boy hadn't thought it through. He couldn't have been more than eighteen and had survived battles that many seasoned soldiers hadn't during his time in South Africa, but in many ways, he was still very much a boy with a child's belief in absolutes. Everything was black and white with no shades of grey in between. In his mind, she was a witch and, therefore, evil. Roger was his commanding officer and a man of nobility and, therefore, could do no wrong.

She almost envied him the certainty he felt. It was something she'd never felt. She'd never been sure of anything in her life until now. For the first time in her life, she was sure of something. She would never leave that farm alive.

That belief was reinforced as they pulled her from her cage, dragged her to a tree at the edge of a clearing and tied her to it. They pulled her arms back and made her face forward. The ancient bark of the tree rubbed against the fabric of her filth-stained dress and cut into her back. They then wrapped iron chains around her and the tree. Her heart sank ever deeper as she watched them drape a hangman's noose over a thick branch above her head as a sick reminder of what they had in store for her.

Roger sat on a tree stump, drinking grog from a metal mug and staring at her. A victorious smile played on his lips. She'd never seen him looking that satisfied during their marriage. Not even after he'd taken his belt to her in their bedroom and done every depraved thing he could think of did he look that pleased with himself.

"Your Captain won't save you this time," he said softly, almost as though he were talking to himself. She had to strain to hear his words. He glugged down what was left of his grog and placed the mug gently on the ground next to his stump as he stood.

"What have you done to him?" Maretta asked as she tried to wriggle out of her bonds, but the futility of the exercise became abundantly clear when she only succeeded in cutting her back against the tree and chaffing her wrists.

"I haven't done anything to your new lover," Roger said with a frown. "More's the pity if truth be told. I would love to knock that look of moral superiority off his distinguished face, but his Lordship seems rather fond of him, and while he might turn a blind eye on a witch being disposed of, he would draw the line at the Captain meeting an untimely death. I thought about demanding satisfaction, but I've seen him on the battlefield, and I'm loathe to admit, I'd probably lose in a duel."

"Really," Maretta said. "You, a coward? Who would have thought."

"I'm not a coward," Roger said as he strode at her.

"Of course not, Dear," Maretta said with a smirk. "You're such a strong, brave man who slaughters helpless civilians and keeps his wife in a cage for months and then ties her to a tree with the help of ten armed men. So very brave of you."

"Say what you wish, my love," Roger said with a grin. "Nothing you say will change the outcome. These men know what you are and will reap their heavenly rewards for ridding the world of yet another one of Satan's legions."

The sound of leaves rustling, followed by a roar, interrupted Roger from saying anything else. The lioness sprang into the clearing, breathing fire.

"We've been waiting for you," Roger said as he pulled a pistol out from behind his back and pointed it at the lioness, who growled in response. The men, whom Maretta thought were drunk and napping, fell into action.

The foot soldier, John, came running with his bayonet attached to his rifle. Instead of firing at her, he ran screaming and tried to impale the lioness, who exhaled a ball of fire into his face. The boy's battle cry turned into howls of pain as he was engulfed in flames and ran with unseeing eyes into the dry bushveld, which caught fire around him as he flailed around, trying to put the fire out. A shot rang out, silencing the boy's screams in an instant. The fire spread, burning the long, dry grass in its wake.

"Jameson," Roger shouted. "Be a good chap and put that fire out while the rest of us deal with this infernal familiar."

"Yes, sir," said another young soldier Maretta recognised from the aftermath of Magersfontein. He'd been one of the men standing with Roger, declaring her a witch. He'd never conversed with her or ascertained her character for himself. He'd taken Roger's words as gospel.

The rest of Roger's men began to circle the lioness, their pistols at the ready, aimed at her head and chest. She seemed to sense what they were doing. Before they could fully encircle her, she pounced at the man closest to her, ripped his throat out and eviscerated the man's stomach. Shots rang out, and the sulphurous odour of gunpowder clung to the air. The lioness was gone when the smoke cleared from the volley of shots. A trail of blood led off into the veld but veered away from where Jameson still struggled to get the blaze under control.

"MacDougal," Roger shouted. "Hunt that beast down and make sure she's dead."

"Yes, sir," MacDougal replied as he slung his rifle over his shoulder and ran after the wounded cat.

"The rest of you, go help Jameson put out that fire. We don't want anyone thinking we need help, now do we," Roger ordered.

"Yes, sir," they all said in unison.

"Now that we've dispatched your familiar and your Captain has been held up by the parade," Roger said as he walked towards her. "Today, my dear, you shall face the divine justice that befalls those who consort with the forces of darkness. The purification of your tainted soul begins now, for your sins as a witch will be cleansed by the fire of God's judgment."

"How do you know that you've truly killed my familiar?" Maretta asked. "If I'm as powerful as you seem to think I am, why would a few bullets do her any real damage?"

"We crafted our bullets specifically for this task," Roger said. "MacDougal comes from a long line of witch-hunters from the Highlands. He knew about your family and how to craft the bullets from iron and witches' salt. Once he's tracked her down, if she isn't dead already, she soon will be, and so will you."

The sound of approaching footsteps came from behind her as Roger nodded. The iron chains were loosened, and rough hands gripped her.

"Let me go, you heartless bastards," Maretta cried as Jameson and the other soot-stained and sweaty men dragged her to the spot under the noose. "Do you have no humanity left in you?"

"You call me heartless," Roger said with a humourless laugh as they pulled the noose over her head. "That is rich coming from you. The woman who promised to love another for all eternity on the very day she made her wedding vows to me."

"How often do I have to tell you before you believe me? Alistair was simply a childhood friend, nothing more," Maretta said as she tried to struggle against the iron cuffs that were once again clamped around her wrists. "I was never unfaithful to you."

"I have your letters to your beloved Alistair and his letters to you. I know everything, my darling unfaithful wife," Roger said as he brandished a piece of parchment that had been read and refolded many times over and appeared stained with what Maretta assumed were drops of blood. "I have here his final words to you, written the day he died. Your lies won't save you."

"What did you do to him?" Maretta screamed as the crushing weight of sorrow enveloped her, and the rope was pulled tight around her throat.

"I was cruelly robbed of that particular satisfaction by a bloody Boer sniper long before we got to these shores," Roger said with a smile. "You've been chasing ghosts, my dear. Perhaps you'll meet each other in hell." He nodded, and his men pulled the rope. Maretta's feet dangled in the air. "But at least the pleasure of seeing you doing the hangman's jig was not denied me."

As Maretta's vision began to blur, she watched as Roger lit a match and burned Alistair's final words to her. She would never know what he'd said to her on those pages or his final thoughts. She only hoped he'd be waiting for her on the other side when she left her mortal coil.

The last sounds she heard as her final breath escaped her lips were Roger's laughter and her grandmother's voice whispering that she would never see Alistair again, that she was a damned disappointment. The voices of her ancestors cursed her to watch over Eithne for all eternity, forever trapped between worlds with no escape.

BOUND BY BETRAYAL

Eithne woke up in the arms of a Nuckelavee and a Banshee. Despite the pounding headache, she smiled at the memory of the night before. It was undoubtedly an experience she'd never thought she'd have, especially considering that both were more likely to kill than spend a night in wild debauchery. She hadn't even known the things they'd done to her were even possible, let alone be toe-curlingly pleasurable.

"I can't even look at you," Maretta said from a chair in the corner of the room.

"You didn't have to stay and watch," Eithne said as she disentangled herself from the cuddle puddle. The Banshee's naked body still glistened from sweat and other fluids that Eithne couldn't quite identify or remember where they'd been excreted from.

"I didn't have a choice," Maretta said. "I'm stuck wherever you are, remember, and with the way you three were carrying on, I didn't have the option of looking in any direction because you were in every corner of the fucking room."

"Fucking room," the Nuckelavee repeated with a tired laugh. "It certainly was that."

"We're supposed to be finding Cailleach, not getting wasted and shagging monsters," Maretta said as she crossed her arms and ignored the laughing Nuckelavee, who was showing off his hard cock.

"You're starting to sound more and more like Thandi, and they're not monsters," Eithne said. "And, clearly, you were too busy disapproving, or you would have heard that they saw Cailleach a few centuries ago fighting with Brigid in the forest on the way to Cailleach's hut after the poetry incident."

"Oh," Maretta said.

"I also know where Cailleach's hut is," Eithne said as she tugged her jeans over her hips.

"Don't go," the Banshee said. "Stay with us. We can have so much fun together."

"Tempting," Eithne said with a sigh and finished getting dressed. "But there are answers to be found and vengeance to be taken before I can satisfy your lust again."

"That is understandable," the Nuckelavee said, and the Banshee nodded.

"Have fun wreaking havoc," the Banshee said with a smile.

"I'll return once my hands have been washed in the blood of my enemies," Eithne said with a backward glance and blew them a kiss.

She blinked at the bright sunshine as she opened the door and left the hut.

"And I thought you didn't want your rage to control you?" Maretta said.

"I don't," Eithne said. "I want to control it and point it all at the person responsible for everything that has happened to me."

"But she's dead," Maretta said. "Has been for almost as long as you were in that box."

"Are you absolutely certain of that?" Eithne asked. "How did she die? Have any of your ancestral spirits seen her spectral form? Have you ever spoken to her in your conversation with your ancestors?"

"Well ... No," Maretta stammered.

"As the last guardian responsible for keeping me imprisoned, don't you find it a little strange that you haven't so much as spoken to her, especially given your recent failure to keep me buried?"

"To be honest, I haven't spoken to any of my ancestors since you rose," Maretta said. "They've been even more silent than usual, which, to be honest, does frighten me a little."

"I see," Eithne said as she picked up her pace.

"I don't think you do. They've ignored me since I died and cursed me. The last time I heard from my mother was just after she died, and it wasn't a particularly pleasant conversation. It was mostly about what a disappointment I was to her and the entire family. I only get snippets of conversations every couple of decades, but mostly they bitch and moan about the state of the world."

Eithne grunted in response.

"Where are we going?" Maretta asked.

"First, we need to find Thandi and Taranis," Eithne said, looking around the grove and at the various huts and witch's cottages spread out around her. "I vaguely remember Thandi fighting with a short guy with green skin, or did I imagine that?"

"You didn't imagine that," Maretta said. "The short green guy was apparently her ex."

"Really?" Eithne said. "I expected him to be tall, muscular, and certainly not green."

"It was a bit of a surprise. I must admit," Maretta said. "Not what I'd pictured at all, either."

"And Taranis?" Eithne asked.

"He was drinking at the bar with a leprechaun, of all things, when we left with those two new friends of yours," Maretta said as she floated behind Eithne, who strode towards Bacchus' Temple.

Taranis sat on a step, stroking Thandi in her lioness form, her head resting in his lap.

"Don't ask," he said as they approached.

"I'm not interested," Eithne said. "I know where Cailleach's hut is."

"So do I," Taranis said. "It's deep in the forest, and no one has seen her in at least two hundred years."

"That matches with the information I have," Eithne said. "We should get going. It's going to be a long walk."

"What's the rush?" Taranis asked.

"I can't explain it, but I know we need to get to her hut, and the sooner we get there, the sooner we'll find something," Eithne said.

"Find what?" Maretta asked.

"I don't know," Eithne said with a frustrated sigh. "I just know we have to get there. It's just an incredibly annoying feeling that's pulling me there. I don't know how else to explain it."

Thandi swished her tail and rolled off Taranis' lap. A small round scar was visible on her right hind leg as she dashed into the forest.

"I never noticed that scar before," Maretta said. "I owe her an apology, don't I?"

Taranis shrugged and followed Thandi into the forest.

"I was trapped in a box when you three had your little adventure, so I don't know what happened or if you owe her an apology for anything," Eithne said. "But right now, if you're done worrying about Thandi's feelings, can we get moving?"

"I go where you go, so the only reason we're still here is that you're not walking," Maretta said. "Perhaps you need to ask why you're stuck to the spot and not running after them."

Eithne sighed as she looked towards the forest.

"I'm afraid of what we might find there," Eithne said. "We might already be too late."

"There's only one way you're ever going to find out, and you only get the answers you need if you move your arse right now."

With trepidation and a sense that dangerous shadows lurked behind every tree, Eithne sighed and started walking towards the darkest part of the forest and Cailleach's hut.

20

Maretta floated next to the tree and watched, unable to do or say anything as they cut the rope, and her body hit the ground with a thump.

"Burn her," Roger said to his remaining men. "Just leave the tree intact. I want to be able to see it and be reminded of what we did here today."

The men nodded and got to work collecting wood. MacDougal hadn't returned in physical form, but she had felt his spirit scream and seen a flash of red light in the distance where she assumed he'd been. That was the last she'd felt of him. But there were other spirits who felt ancient and wise drifting around the clearing. They seemed to be waiting for something. She knew from their silence and lack of interest in her that they were waiting for something or someone else. She felt it as well. Eithne was close by.

She wanted to kick and scream as they built a pyre and flung her body on top of it as though she was nothing. Jameson doused her body in paraffin, and Roger struck the match that set her physical form ablaze. A part of her was grateful they'd hanged her first. They could have burned her at the stake like some of her ancestors had been.

Roger smiled as he watched the fire turn her into ash. Only when the fire died, and there was nothing but ash left of her, Roger and his men mounted their horses and rode away.

It didn't take long for the wagon carrying Eithne to come from the opposite direction. The Captain sat tall in the front seat. His bloody hands gripped the reigns tightly. He pulled the wagon to a halt, where the wind slowly took her pyre's ashes. He climbed into the back of the wagon and returned carrying the wounded lioness, who slowly returned to her human form in his arms.

"You didn't need to save me," the young girl whispered. "I had that savage right where I wanted him."

"I know," the Captain said. "A Goddess of war is even more ferocious when wounded and certainly doesn't need to be saved by the God of Thunder in a fight."

"Precisely," the girl said as he gently placed her on the ground, carefully placing her on the side that wasn't wounded. "But I am grateful for your assistance and care, Taranis."

"As always, Sekhmet," Taranis said with a smile and a bow. "I'm ever your humble servant."

"Humble?" Sekhmet said with a chuckle. "Please don't make me laugh. It still smarts a little."

"It'll heal once I remove the bullet," Taranis said as he knelt beside her. "This might sting a little."

Sekhmet inhaled sharply as he extracted the bullet and cauterised the wound with tiny lightning bolts.

"What do we do now that the last guardian is dead?" Sekhmet asked as she stood. "Can we finally set her free?"

"Only an innocent can free her," Taranis said as he walked to the back of the wagon and pulled out two spades. Handing one to Sekhmet, he began to dig a grave where Maretta's body had been burned.

"And what of Maretta's spirit?" Sekhmet asked. "Why is she still here? Why hasn't she joined her family?"

"I don't have all the answers," Taranis said. "She was the last of her line, after all. Perhaps her fate is to keep watch over Eithne in death as well."

"The fates are cruel," Sekhmet said.

"Perhaps," Taranis said as he lowered the Kist into the grave. "Or perhaps she still has a greater role to play. Only time will tell."

"What will you do now?" Sekhmet asked.

"I'm going back to my cottage in the Highlands," he sighed. "I miss my books and research, and when I get bored, I think I'll pay the Lieutenant a visit and take my time making him suffer, and then there are Maretta's brothers and the rest of her family that must be dealt with. They can't be allowed to have any more daughters. And you? What will you do now?"

"I'm going to stay in this city and wait," Sekhmet said. "I think I'll change my name. Perhaps live amongst the humans for a while, and when she wakes up, I'll be ready for her."

"When she does, will you bring her to me?" Taranis said. "She'll have questions and might need me."

Sekhmet nodded and turned back into her cat form. After one last glance at Maretta's spirit, she ran into the veld.

"I'm sorry," Taranis said as he climbed back into the wagon and left Maretta alone with the silent spirits who drifted to Eithne's grave, forming a procession as they paid their respects one by one and then drifted away. Soon, they were all gone, and only Maretta was left to stand sentinel and wait for the day when someone came to release Eithne.

Cailleach's hut was dilapidated, and Deadly Nightshade had taken the building hostage. The forest surrounding it was strangely quiet. No birds chirped, and even the cicadas were silent. Only a lone raven sat perched on a branch, watching them. Thandi's lioness form prowled the area. Her tail swished from side to side as she sniffed the air.

"Something terrible happened here," Taranis said, stating the obvious.

"No shit," Thandi said as she transformed into her human form.

Eithne strode towards the hut without a word and began pulling the Nightshade away from the door in a frantic rush while the others stood back and allowed Eithne her space to work through her emotions. Once she'd cleared the Nightshade out of the way, she kicked the door. The rotten wood splintered into pieces, allowing her to enter what she could only think of as a crime scene.

Furniture was turned over, and weathered scorch marks adorned the cracked and aged wooden walls and floors. There'd been a violent struggle. But there were no clues as to who had won the fight, nor was there any sign of Cailleach. The lack of life was also evident inside the cottage. After standing empty for so long, Eithne expected to see at least a few spiderwebs in corners or on the furniture, but there weren't any. Not even a cockroach scuttled out of the light from the open doorway.

"Whatever happened here," Taranis said. "I know she survived it. I would have felt it if she'd been killed."

"Luckily, killing us is almost impossible," Thandi said.

"There are worse things than death for an immortal," Eithne said.

"True," Thandi said with an almost imperceptible shiver.

"Only an incredibly powerful being would be able to have attacked Cailleach, caused this kind of damage, and survived," Taranis said as he looked around the cottage and examined bits of debris.

"It's a very short list," Thandi said. "I doubt any of the creatures here would have been capable of this."

"What about Brigid?" Maretta asked. "Everyone said they saw them fighting."

"Brigid would never attack anyone physically," Taranis said. "It's not in her nature. It's more likely for Cailleach to attack her. In which case, Brigid would have been the one either missing or dead."

"But then who?" Maretta asked. "Who would want to harm her?"

"She did have a tendency of pissing other immortals off," Thandi said. "She wasn't the friendliest of Goddesses. Then there was her tendency to interfere in matters that some probably felt weren't her business."

"Cailleach may be bad-tempered, but they all respect her too much to do this," Taranis said. "They tend to just leave her alone, and most don't care enough about the human world to worry about what Cailleach does or doesn't interfere in, and she hasn't interfered in important matters in millennia. She'd retreated from the world."

"Is it just me," Maretta said. "But does it almost feel as though she was hiding here?"

"Well," Thandi said. "Whatever she was hiding from found her."

"You're being very quiet," Taranis said to Eithne, who had picked up a burnt piece of wood and was staring at it, lost in thought.

"This is a dead end," Eithne said. "There are no answers here, only more questions."

"So, what do you propose we do?" Taranis asked.

"Nothing," Eithne said as she threw the piece of wood back onto the floor.

"What the fuck do you mean, nothing?" Thandi asked.

"Just that," Eithne said. "Nothing. You go back to your shop, Taranis returns to his cottage and books, and we go back to Nick's apartment. If he's still alive, I should probably feed him."

"I don't understand," Thandi said. "Are you giving up already?"

Eithne smiled and glanced toward the broken window where the lone crow stood on the windowsill watching them.

"You're right," Taranis said with a nod. "We should go home. There's nothing here."

"I don't understand," Maretta said.

"Come along, dumbass," Thandi said. "I'll explain when we get back to the portal."

Taranis and Eithne left Cailleach's hut without a backward glance and strolled down the trail through the forest with Thandi and Maretta close behind.

They only stopped once they reached the portal and ensured the crow hadn't followed them out of the forest.

"So," Thandi said. "Now that we're no longer being watched. What's the actual plan?"

"As I said," Eithne said. "We do nothing. We go home, and we wait."

"You think whoever took Cailleach will come for us," Taranis said.

"Yes," Eithne said.

"But whoever did that to Cailleach is incredibly powerful," Maretta said. "We can't possibly defend ourselves against that on our own."

"Who said anything about being on our own?" Eithne said.

"I know some creatures back in the city who might come in handy," Thandi said with a smile.

"I thought you might," Eithne said.

"Okay," Maretta said. "I'm already dead, so it's not like I can be killed all over again, right?"

"Right," Taranis said with a smile. "Let's go home."

As Eithne stepped through the portal, she couldn't help but wonder how long it would take before whoever or whatever was behind Cailleach's disappearance revealed themselves. How long would she have to wait for the answers to her creation, and was she right about Mael Muire being alive? Could she be the elusive puppeteer behind it all?

The only thing Eithne knew for sure was that the next move belonged to whoever had been watching them through the eyes of that cunning crow. The puzzle, a labyrinthine tapestry of intrigue and mystery, had only just begun to unravel, and Eithne was determined to see it through to its inevitable bloody conclusion. Eithne knew blood would be spilt no matter who emerged victorious at the end of it all.

The End

For now

Eithne and Maretta will be back in their next adventure.

Thank you for taking the time out of your busy day to read my words.

Did you enjoy the book?

Here's what you can do next.

If you loved the book and have a few seconds to spare, please leave a review wherever you bought it.

Your help in spreading the word is very much appreciated.

Be a Freaky Darling

Would you like to read a sharp, brutal zombie romp spiced with humour? Would you like it for free?
Be a Freaky Darling!

Subscribe to my newsletter and get a copy of Oasis, along with all sorts of freebies and surprises.
For more information, visit www.joandelahaye.com.

Acknowledgements

Eileen, my big sister, thanks for teaching me to read and giving me a love of the written word.

Thanks, Mom – for everything!

Simoné, the Ginger Ninja, thank you for letting me bounce story ideas and titles off you at inconvenient times. For dealing with my insecurities about every single aspect of writing and publishing efforts, and most of all, thank you for making sure Bound by Betrayal doesn't suck.

Marlene, my sister from another mister. You are my rock and head cheerleader. Your constant support keeps me going when all I want to do is give up. Thank you!

About the Author

Joan De La Haye writes horror, dark fantasy and some very twisted thrillers. She invariably wakes up in the middle of the night because she's figured out yet another freaky way to mess with her already screwed-up characters.

Joan is interested in some seriously weird stuff. That's probably also one of the reasons she writes horror.

You can stalk Joan on her website: www.joandelahaye.com

Fury

Embark on a chilling journey into the heart of South Africa's capital city, where two rival crime bosses engage in a brutal battle for supremacy, leaving the underground film industry in ruins. In "Fury" by Joan De La Haye, an enraged spirit unleashes a reign of terror, seeking vengeance through a relentless and murderous rampage. Caught in the midst of this violent conflict is Alice, a university student fighting for her very survival.

Experience a twisted tale of revenge that will linger in your nightmares as Alice desperately struggles to escape the clutches of this malevolent force. Will she triumph over the wrathful entity or become another casualty in its path of destruction?

Acclaimed by critics, "Fury" by Joan De La Haye captivates with its intelligent storytelling, flawless pacing, and expert execution. Prepare yourself for a bone-chilling narrative where the destinies of various characters intertwine, and the fury of the vengeful spirit reigns supreme.

Praise for "Fury":

"A twisted tale of revenge that will haunt your dreams." – Paul Simpson, Sci-Fi Bulletin

"Smart, perfectly paced, and well executed... you just can't beat a REALLY angry ghost." – The Eloquent Page.

Requiem in E Sharp

Immerse yourself in the heart-pounding thriller, "Requiem in E Sharp" by Joan De La Haye. Set against the backdrop of South Africa's capital city, Pretoria, this captivating story follows a troubled detective locked in a deadly dance with a tormented serial killer. Brace yourself for a world where carefully selected women fall victim to a murderer haunted by a chilling past.

As the sadistic spree of The Bathroom Strangler escalates, Detective Nico van Staaden races against time, battling not only the relentless killer but also his own personal demons. With seemingly unrelated murders intertwining in a treacherous labyrinth, Nico faces mounting pressure from his superiors, amplifying the urgency of his mission.

Prepare for a heart-stopping climax, an eruption of bloodshed, brutality, and a merciless reckoning. Will Nico prevail against an enemy whose twisted psyche knows no bounds, or will he succumb to the deadly symphony orchestrated by the Bathroom Strangler?

"Requiem in E Sharp" is a spine-chilling thriller that will leave you breathless, gripping the edge of your seat until the very last nerve-wracking note. Joan De La Haye skillfully crafts a tale of suspense, psychological torment, and the delicate balance between good and evil. Embark on a gripping journey into the depths of the human soul, where redemption and vengeance collide in an explosive crescendo of violence. Get ready for an unforgettable exploration of the darkest recesses of the human psyche.

Oasis

Experience the relentless horror of a post-apocalyptic world in "Oasis," a gripping and darkly satisfying zombie novella that delves into themes of resilience, horror, and the unyielding human will to survive.

In the wake of devastating solar flares, the remaining population has been transformed into flesh-craving zombies due to solar radiation, leaving only a handful of survivors unscathed.

A resilient family of civilians and a battle-hardened squad of soldiers are on a desperate mission to reach the safety of New Atlantis, a fortified UN base at the South Pole. With hordes of undead relentlessly pursuing them, their harrowing journey becomes a desperate race against time. Will they manage to reach the oasis of New Atlantis alive, or will they succumb to the ravenous undead and join their ranks?

Praise for Oasis:

"Oasis treads classic Romero-esque ground and has a suitably downbeat ending that I really enjoyed. I have to admit I do enjoy my zombie stories to be grimmer than grim and I'm glad to say this novella delivers on that score." – The Eloquent Page.

"OASIS is sharp, brutal, spiced with humour, and a great addition to the ever-growing sub-genre of Zombie Apocalypse tales. It stands on its own and yet again showcases Joan's great talents with words and storytelling. If you're looking for a quick read that'll give you thrills, terror and zombies..." – Dave de Burgh.

Burning

She thought she could summon a lover but got a demon instead.

Experience a sizzling collision of magic and desire in the captivating paranormal novella, "Burning," written by Joan De La Haye. When the lonely witch, Marcie Grove, grows weary of her dismal love life, she dares to summon a lover through a transformative full moon ritual. Little does she know that her desperate attempt to find romance will ignite a perilous encounter with a malevolent demon, threatening not only her existence but also the lives of her coven members. As the chilling consequences unravel with explosive intensity, "Burning" immerses readers in a scorching tale of dark desires and mystical mayhem.

Step into a twisted world and prepare to be ensnared in an inferno of suspense and supernatural intrigue that will leave you spellbound.

Praise for "Burning":

"Verdict: A horror story that uses its eroticism to chilling effect. 8/10" – Sci-Fi Bulletin

"Worth every minute and great for a commute, lunch break or time for yourself." – Horror Blog.

The Race

Experience the electrifying thrill of survival in "The Race," the heart-pounding first instalment of Joan De La Haye's gripping series. Follow Joanna Perry, an unsuspecting victim thrust into a world where life hangs in the balance, as she embarks on an unimaginable journey.

When Joanna's life takes a terrifying turn, she finds herself drugged, violently abducted and forced into a deadly contest for the entertainment of the world's elite. With her own survival on the line, she must confront her limits in a twisted game orchestrated by the rich and depraved.

As the stakes reach unprecedented heights, Joanna must tap into her inner strength and navigate treacherous terrain where each step could be her last. Will she embrace her newfound ferocity and outsmart her merciless adversaries, or will she succumb to the darkness that surrounds her?

"The Race" delivers an adrenaline-fueled narrative that will leave readers breathless. With its breakneck pace and relentless action, this quick read is a perfect fit for fans of pulse-pounding tales like "The Hunger Games," "Gladiator," and "The Running Man." Brace yourself for a rollercoaster ride of danger, courage, and the fight for freedom.

Enter a world where survival is the ultimate triumph, where glory exacts a deadly cost, and the race for Joanna's life, glory, and gold brook no mercy. Get ready for an adventure that will keep you on the edge of your seat until the very last page.

Sliced and Diced

Embark on a thrilling journey through the dark and twisted imagination of author Joan De La Haye as she presents a captivating collection of tales that will both fascinate and disturb you.

Within these pages, Joan De La Haye invites you to explore a sinister world where the line between reality and nightmare blurs. Join a relentless serial killer as he hunts for his next trophy, feeling the chill of his calculated pursuit. Witness the chilling reunion of vengeful ghosts driven by an insatiable hunger for vengeance that transcends death itself. Feel the raw intensity of jealousy as a girlfriend takes a sinister turn, extinguishing her lover's beloved pet. Encounter a ghost bride and a tormenting demon whose presence sends shivers down the spines of even the most resilient.

While some of these gripping narratives have been previously celebrated in acclaimed anthologies, others are unveiled here for the very first time. Joan De La Haye's mastery of storytelling guarantees a mesmerising experience that will thrill, shock, and disturb you. Just remember to keep the lights on as you immerse yourself in these chilling tales that will leave an indelible mark on your psyche.

Sliced and Diced 2

Immerse yourself in the sinister imagination of author Joan De La Haye as she unleashes a captivating collection of 13 dark and twisted tales in her second collection. Brace yourself for a rollercoaster ride of suspense as each story explores the depths of human nature and the supernatural.

Uncover the harrowing tale of a hunter turned hunted, where the line between predator and prey becomes blurred. Witness a diabolical wedding as the Devil himself takes a bride, plunging the world into chaos. Prepare for mayhem when a malevolent typewriter wreaks havoc on unsuspecting inhabitants of an old house, its sinister secrets coming to life.

Join forces with the Devil's PR agent as they navigate a treacherous path to bring a killer to justice, their actions revealing the darkness lurking in the shadows. And dare to explore the true cost of real estate in Hell, where deals with the devil come with unimaginable consequences.

With Joan De La Haye's masterful storytelling, each tale will send shivers down your spine and keep you on the edge of your seat. These captivating narratives promise thrills and chills that will leave you breathless, but be warned: the darkness within is best confronted with the comforting glow of light. Prepare to embark on a journey that will test your courage and haunt your dreams long after you've turned the final page.

Sliced and Diced 3

Embark on a chilling journey into the depths of darkness with acclaimed author Joan De La Haye as she presents another gripping collection of 13 dark and twisted tales. From the deceptive allure of a lucky coin to the haunting disappearance of a lost child in the woods, each story will leave you questioning the fragility of your reality.

Join a couple on a seemingly innocent hike, only to discover that their greatest threat lies not in infidelity but in something far more sinister. Stand alongside an old woman as she fiercely defends herself and her faithful companion against unspeakable horrors. Uncover the secrets of a mysterious gateway that opens doors to a world where forbidden knowledge brings dire consequences.

Joan De La Haye's masterful storytelling delves deep into the shadows, stirring a potent blend of suspense, horror, and unease. These 13 captivating narratives will disturb your nights as the lines between dreams and nightmares blur. Be forewarned: the monsters lurking within these pages are best kept at bay by the comforting glow of light.

As you immerse yourself in each tale, prepare for a thrilling and thought-provoking experience that will linger long after you've turned the final page. Joan De La Haye's dark visions will test the limits of your imagination, keeping you on edge and reminding you that sometimes the most terrifying monsters are the ones that dwell within our own minds.

Shadows

Delve into the depths of psychological terror and uncover the chilling secrets shrouding Sarah's tormented existence in "Shadows" by Joan De La Haye. This haunting horror novel will captivate your soul, leaving you questioning reality and your sanity until the bone-chilling revelation that awaits you.

Sarah teeters on the precipice of madness as the ghosts of her family's dark past relentlessly haunt her. Plagued by violent, blood-drenched hallucinations, she seeks help from her trusted psychologist and confidant, Michael Brink.

Within Sarah's treacherous battle to reclaim her sanity, she stumbles upon a realm far more sinister than she could have ever imagined. Her relentless pursuit for answers thrusts her into a nightmarish confrontation with a demon hell-bent on torment and death—a terror that feeds on her deepest fears.

Praise for "Shadows":

"If you're open to reading a book that is genuinely disturbing, in some cases distasteful, and creepy as hell, then I'm pretty sure you'll 'enjoy' Shadows." - Dave de Burgh, author of Betrayal's Shadow.

"Dark, twisted and creepy, Shadows will take you out of your comfort zone and keep you glued to the pages of the book, regardless of whether or not you want to." - Tammy February, W24.

Prepare to question your sanity as you embark on Sarah's quest for truth. "Shadows" will seize your imagination, leaving an indelible mark long after you turn the final page. Dare to confront the darkness within.

The Veil

Sarah's worst nightmare resurfaces with an unstoppable vengeance in "The Veil," the gripping sequel by Joan De La Haye. Brace yourself for a harrowing descent into a world consumed by relentless terror as the malevolent force she once believed defeated, Jack, returns to torment her existence.

In this chilling continuation of the Diabolical Series, Joan De La Haye thrusts us back into the darkness where Sarah thought she had escaped. The sinister presence of Jack lurks in the shadows, haunting her life with a renewed malevolence and chilling determination. But Jack is not alone this time; a legion of evil accompanies him, preying upon the vulnerabilities of Sarah's unsuspecting friends.

As the line between reality and nightmare blurs once more, the stakes escalate to unprecedented heights. Prepare yourself for a spine-chilling journey where the horrors of the past surge forth with unrelenting fury. Joan De La Haye weaves a web of suspense and terror, leaving you breathless and compelled to uncover the fate of Sarah and her companions.

Can you confront the malevolent forces that await beyond "The Veil"? The relentless darkness looms, and Jack's insidious presence threatens to consume everything in its path. Immerse yourself in this gripping sequel that will seize hold of your imagination, leaving you trembling long after you've turned the final page. Dare to face your deepest fears within "The Veil."

Milton Keynes UK
Ingram Content Group UK Ltd.
UKHW041030260124
436746UK00004B/156

9 798223 463689